The town of Millbrook needed a new shopping center; everyone was in agreement about that. But why did the new center have to be built on what had been the Little League baseball field?

Kit Dawson and his friends faced a long, empty summer without baseball unless somehow a playing field could be found for them.

Then Kit, who knew nothing about old people but thought he didn't like them very much, found himself visiting in a retirement home. Kit thought that the old people were annoyed by his visit; but shortly afterward, he discovered that the members of the home had offered their grounds to the Little League as a playing field.

However, they stipulated that there was to be no undue noise. Can you imagine a baseball game with no cheering when the first homer is swatted in?

Playing games in ghostly silence was bad enough, but Kit was convinced that the old people were even a bigger jinx than the number thirteen on his uniform. All he had to do to flub a play was to look up and see one of their faces. He could tell by their expressions that they were being critical of him and his friends.

Don Creighton's account of the ball games that were played that summer on the grounds of the retirement home makes exciting reading for sports fans. But *Little League Old-Timers* is also written on a much deeper level, for the author explores the tensions and misunderstandings that mar relationships between the generations—children, parents, and even older persons. The story shows the reader that if the old and the young can learn to understand each other better, the lives of both are enriched.

Don Creighton's previous books, *Little League Giant* and *The Secret Little Leaguer*, were warmly welcomed by readers and reviewers alike. The author has been praised for an excellent writing style and fine understanding of human nature.

LITTLE LEAGUE OLD-TIMERS

LITTLE LEAGUE
OLD-TIMERS

by DON CREIGHTON

Steck-Vaughn Company
Austin, Texas

Chapter 1

An Empty Summer

"WHAT A ROTTEN SUMMER this is going to be!" Twelve-year-old Kit Dawson scowled and dug his fists deeper into his pockets.

"How could they do it to us? It's not fair." Slim, freckle-faced Tom Fairbanks shook his head mournfully.

Tony Sheldon, tallest of the three and as heavy as Kit and Tom put together, shrugged his shoulders and sighed. "They don't care whether it's fair or not," he said. "You think they care about *us?*"

The boys were gazing mournfully at what was left of the Millbrook Little League field. There wasn't much to see. The backstop was gone and so was the outfield fence. The bleachers had been taken down, as well as all but a couple of the big trees that had for many seasons shaded fans from the summer heat. What used to be second base had

5

already been gobbled up by a big steam shovel that was eating away the earth in the direction of the pitcher's mound.

"Who needs a new shopping center, anyway?" Kit demanded scornfully.

Tony's face reddened. "My father's moving in as soon as it's finished. He says the town really needs one bad."

"I guess so," Tom agreed. "Last time we needed some paint, my father wanted to buy it at your father's store. But he couldn't find a parking place, so we drove over to Bridgeton for it."

"Maybe we do need a shopping center," Kit admitted. "But why does it have to be here? They are taking our field just when our biggest year is coming up."

"That's right," Tom sighed. "It won't make much difference to the younger kids. They're sure to find a place to play by next season, and they'll have another chance. But not us. We're the old-timers in the league. Next year we'll be thirteen and too old."

"We'll be gypped," Kit mourned. "And the Colts will be gypped worst of all. It was bad enough winding up last season in the cellar. But we all figured we'd be lots better this year. Now we'll never have a chance to prove it."

Tony summed it up. "It just goes to show that nobody cares about kids. It's the old people that

6

run things, and the older they get the less they care."

Conversations much like this were going on every day all over Millbrook. None of the Little League players could understand why the field they had always thought belonged to them had been taken away. Even when they had been forced to accept that fact, they couldn't understand why there wasn't some other place for them. What was wrong with the school playing fields?

"It's explained right here in the *Journal*," Kit's father told him patiently, after he had asked that question for about the twentieth time. "The small children need the elementary school playgrounds for their summer day camp. And the field at the high school is used by the Babe Ruth League and the American Legion team. It wouldn't be fair to deprive other people of their pleasure, would it?"

"I suppose not." But Kit was sure that nothing was as important as Little League. It seemed to him that the little children could play in their own yards and that the big boys could find something else to do. He didn't want to sound selfish, so he gave his father the answer he wanted, then added stubbornly, "There must be some other place."

Mr. Dawson shook his head. "I only wish there were. You know I'm on the League's Board of Directors this year, and I can tell you that everyone on the board is as anxious as you to get in the season's play. Why, Millbrook was the first town in this area to organize a Little League. A lot of us have worked hard these twelve years to make it bigger and better each season. Do you think we wanted this to happen?"

Kit's eyes widened. "Do you think it's on account of the thirteenth season coming up? Could it be a jinx?"

"Don't be silly! It could have happened any time. The fact is, we're lucky it didn't happen before. The owner of the land has been letting us use it all these years practically for nothing. It's valuable land, too, right in the middle of Millbrook. He finally got an offer he couldn't afford to turn down, and it wouldn't have been right to ask him to. Millbrook needs a new business area with modern buildings and space for parking. That may not seem important to you now, but it will when you're older."

Kit couldn't imagine that ever seeming important. "There must be some place," he repeated.

"You find one, then," his father suggested. "Remember, it has to be near the center of town so that it won't be too hard for the boys to get to. There has to be enough open, reasonably level space to lay out a field. And it has to be far enough away from people's houses so we won't get complaints about windows being broken or babies being kept awake by the noise. If you find a place like that, let me know."

8

"Okay, I will," Kit said. It would be a cinch, Kit thought. There must be thousands of such places in a town the size of Millbrook.

But, amazingly, there were not thousands. After a week in which Kit and his friends walked the streets of Millbrook exploring the town from side to side and from end to end, it began to seem that there wasn't even one.

The boys made some suggestions to Kit's father and some other members of the board, but some sites were too small and others too far away. Some were too hilly or too swampy or covered with trees which the owner wouldn't allow anyone to cut down. A couple which had looked possible had houses so placed that a well-hit ball could hardly have avoided breaking a window.

When spring warmed the air, bats and balls and gloves began to appear on the school grounds and the vacant lots. But their owners used them with none of the enthusiasm they had shown in other years.

"Dad's going to let me help in the store during summer vacation," Tony announced as he met Kit and Tom on Saturday morning. On his round face was the first real smile his friends had seen there in a long time. "We're getting ready to move to the new shopping center, so there'll be plenty of things I can do."

"I talked my parents into letting me go to camp,"

Tom said. "At first they kept saying they couldn't afford it. But they finally decided they could manage somehow, as long as there wouldn't be anything to do here."

"You guys are lucky." Kit knew he should be happy for his friends, but he couldn't manage it. His family had no store for him to work in. And he surely wouldn't be going away to camp. Kit's mother said that she couldn't imagine how parents could stand being separated from their children all summer. That had always been fine with Kit, for he couldn't imagine a nicer place to spend the summer than right at home in Millbrook. But during this empty summer he wouldn't even have his two best friends for company.

There would be nothing to do through all the long, hot days but mourn the death of the Millbrook Little League. What a way to spend what should have been the most exciting summer of his life!

Chapter 2

A House of Mystery

DARKNESS WAS STARTING to fall as Kit called good-bye to Tom and Tony and headed toward home. He slouched along, a bat over his shoulder with his glove looped carelessly over it. His face was gloomy. Pretty bad when even Saturdays weren't any fun, he thought.

The only fun anybody wanted at this time of year was baseball. Kit and his friends had been ready for a day of it. But they had been chased out of the school yard when someone hit a ball too near a bunch of little kids. They had to leave the little park at the top of the hill when a policeman pointed out a sign that said KEEP OFF THE GRASS. They also were driven out of a vacant lot and a wide, inviting street.

Such things had happened in other years, but they hadn't seemed important since the boys had

11

known they would be starting Little League practice soon. This year there was nothing else to look forward to, so each rejection made them angrier and more discouraged.

None of the Millbrook boys seemed able to talk about anything except Little League baseball and how terrible the summer would be without it. Members of the Tigers were sure they could take first place again if they had a chance. Good players, and even some not quite so good, grumbled that it wasn't fair for them to miss a chance to play for the Millbrook All-Stars as their older brothers and friends had done. They just knew that this would have been the year when Millbrook slaughtered all opposition and wound up the season covered with glory.

Kit could have resigned himself to missing his chance to compete for a place on the All-Stars. After all, he had every twelve-year-old in town for company. But he hated to think of how disappointed his parents would be.

Though they had never told him so, Kit knew that his parents expected a lot from him. Being an only child was nice in a way, but it was also a big responsibility. He had no brothers or sisters coming along to make up for his failures. In the Dawson family everything was up to Kit, so he wanted to be best at whatever he did. He wanted his father, who had handed trophies to so many other Little

Leaguers, to be proud that his own son had earned one. He wanted his mother, who had newspaper clippings about every game he had ever played neatly pasted into a scrapbook, to add more to her collection. When he thought of the unfairness of it all, the whole world seemed cold and gloomy.

If this was the way Saturdays were going to be, Kit brooded, he would just as soon not even go out. It would serve the grownups right if all the kids in Millbrook sat home until they became so fat and pale from not getting any exercise or sunshine that they looked like a bunch of toadstools. Maybe then the grown people would be sorry!

After he had enjoyed a moment of laughter over the thought of all those pale, puffy kids and their worried parents, Kit decided it really wouldn't be worthwhile turning into a blob just to get even. Anyway, his parents didn't deserve such treatment. They were doing the best they could, and probably lots of other parents were, too.

If only they could find a place to make a field! Kit hated the thought of giving up, but there didn't seem to be anything else to do. He and his friends had searched up and down every street in Millbrook.

Then Kit stopped short and stared. He suddenly realized that there was one street they hadn't explored. And it was only a few blocks from his home. He passed it every day, yet he had never walked down it.

There was some excuse for that, for the street didn't come from anywhere. It started at Pleasant Avenue, about three blocks from Kit's house. And plainly it didn't go anywhere, for at the corner was a large sign that said NO EXIT. Still, it was a real street that was almost as wide as Pleasant Avenue.

The street seemed darker and emptier than other streets. There were no houses visible along it. The sign on the corner under which Kit was standing said "Marley Place."

Kit stood still, frowning. He couldn't think why he had never gone down Marley Place when he had been everywhere else in town. It was just that he had grown up feeling there was something scary about it. It wasn't the fun-kind of scariness that made kids want to explore. It was the dark, serious kind that made them keep away.

Maybe it was all right for little kids to feel that way, Kit thought. They could believe in witches and goblins and ghosts, could imagine bears or tigers lurking behind every bush. But Kit was twelve years old. Anybody twelve years old knew there couldn't be anything dangerous right in the middle of Millbrook.

Kit passed the NO EXIT sign on the corner and took a few steps into Marley Place. There were still no houses in sight. On both sides next to the walks were fences of stout wire mesh. Tall pine trees grew close together just inside. A short way ahead, the street curved, hiding whatever was beyond.

Kit couldn't imagine anyone making a street that led nowhere. Something was beyond that curve, and Kit couldn't claim to have explored Millbrook completely until he had seen what it was. He had no hope of finding anything useful; but unless he looked, he would never be satisfied.

He took a deep breath and strode determinedly around the bend. A few yards ahead were a pair of closed iron gates that were twice as high as Kit's head. They were made of iron bars which had been bent into fancy designs. Although the gates were closed, it was possible to see between the bars.

Kit went up close and peered through. Straight ahead, a smooth gravel driveway led to a circular turnaround in front of what Kit was sure must be the biggest house in Millbrook. The biggest—and the ugliest, he decided.

A little shudder ran through Kit. When you saw a house like that in the movies or on TV, scary things followed. He imagined hands reaching out from hidden panels, unearthly shrieks, and bodies falling out of closets.

He craned his neck to look to the left. There was a narrow strip of neatly-mown lawn with some benches and chairs arranged along its edges. The benches and chairs were painted black, and all of them were empty.

Looking to the right, Kit saw something that made him catch his breath sharply. Closed in on three sides by tall, closely-growing pine trees was a smooth stretch of lawn that was perfect for a baseball field.

Kit let his imagination decorate the field with bases, with a backstop, and with a pitcher's mound. He added players' benches and some bleachers for spectators. There was room to spare. His heart beat fast, and he was so filled with excitement he didn't even feel the cold roughness of the bars against the side of his face.

"Boy! Boy!" The shrill, raucous voice was like the screeching of a parrot. Down the driveway came a figure dressed in black from the shawl-draped head to the full black skirt fluttering almost to the ground. Kit wanted to run, but his hands seemed frozen to the bars.

"What do you want, boy?" This was a different voice. Kit managed to tear his eyes away from what he would have been sure was a witch if he hadn't known that witches do not exist.

Approaching him from the left, just inside the fence, was another alarming figure. It was very tall and thin. It was dressed in men's clothing, but the garments were so loose and floppy that they seemed to have been made for someone else. Kit thought instantly of a scarecrow.

Kit loosened his terrified grip on the bars. He

turned to run, but something gripped his arm. Kit stood frozen with horror.

Just at his ear, a soft, unearthly chuckle sounded. A wheezy little voice said, "Come in, boy. Tell us what you're looking for."

A moment passed before Kit could force himself to look around in the direction of the voice. Holding his elbow and looking straight into his face was a bent-over little man. He had a large, hooked nose and bushy eyebrows. Straggly white hair hung down from under a broad black hat. He looked exactly like the goblin in one of Kit's old picture books.

Chapter 3

Kit Tells His Story

KIT BRACED HIMSELF for a desperate attempt at escape and almost fell flat when the grip on his arm was suddenly released. Taking a backward step, Kit intended to get well out of the goblin's reach and then make a run for it. He didn't know what was inside that dark, sinister house, and he didn't want to find out.

The goblin had taken a large key from his pocket and was concentrating on inserting it into a massive lock. Kit set himself to whirl and race for the safety of Pleasant Avenue. But first he looked quickly about, just to make sure there were no other witches, scarecrows, or goblins lying in wait. Then his eyes lit on something he should have seen before. He went limp with relief.

On the big stone post beside the gate was a metal plaque. It was partly obscured by the drooping

18

tendril of a vine. Some of its letters were nearly worn away, but once noticed it was easy to read.

THE ELNATHAN F. MARLEY
HOME
FOR THE AGED

Kit realized that he had let his imagination run away with him. The only consolation was that none of his friends had been there to see how scared he had been. Suddenly the house of evil mystery was just a big, old-fashioned house. It wasn't inhabited by witches, scarecrows, and goblins, but by old people.

The gate was open now. Kit passed through, following the old man he still couldn't help thinking of as a goblin. He saw that the scarecrow was just a skinny old man wearing a suit that he must have bought years ago when he was fatter. The witch was an old lady who smiled at him, showing a set of very shiny false teeth.

"Looking for someone, boy?" she asked. Her voice was still harsh and high-pitched, but it sounded friendly.

"No, ma'am."

The scarecrow frowned. "You must be one of those boys that throw candy wrappers and empty bottles over our front wall."

"No, sir," Kit denied earnestly. "I never threw anything over your wall in my whole life."

19

"You were up to something," the scarecrow insisted. "What's in your pockets, boy? Firecrackers? Maybe we'd better telephone the police."

"I wasn't up to anything. Honest, sir!" Kit dropped his bat and glove and started turning out his pockets. They mustn't call the police—his mother would die of shame. A nickel and a few pennies fell out, followed by part of a roll of mints, a couple of baseball cards, a brand-new jackknife, and a broken cigarette lighter.

"So!" the goblin said. "You were going to set fire to something."

"It doesn't work," Kit said hopelessly. "Please try it. You'll see."

The scarecrow flicked the little wheel several times. Then he handed it back to Kit. "You're right. Not much fire hazard there. But how about that knife? Must be one of those switchblades I've read about in the papers."

"No, sir! It's just a regular knife for sharpening pencils and stuff. See?" With trembling hands Kit managed to pry open the stiff new blades.

The old man nodded slowly. "But then what are you doing here?"

"Just passing by," Kit said uncertainly.

"But we're not on the way to anywhere," the witch said. Then in a kinder voice she asked, "What's your name, boy?"

With such a very old lady it seemed best to use

his proper name. "Christopher Dawson, ma'am."

"Well, Christopher, I'm Miss Rogers. This is Mr. McIntyre. And Mr. Benjamin." Kit cautiously shook hands with them.

"Since you're here, Christopher, you must come in and have some refreshments."

That was the last thing Kit wanted to do, but it seemed best to agree. If he refused they might start thinking about the police again. So he walked up the driveway between Mr. McIntyre, the scarecrow, and Mr. Benjamin, the goblin. All followed Miss Rogers through the heavy black doorway.

Inside, the house was warm and stuffy. It smelled of a lot of things, mostly medicine and mothballs. The witch—he must remember to think of her as Miss Rogers, Kit told himself—led the way into a large room where several other old people were sitting.

"Have a chair, Christopher," Miss Rogers invited.

Leaning on her cane, Miss Rogers shuffled out of the room. Mr. Benjamin introduced the other old men and old ladies, and Kit shook hands with them all. It gave him an uneasy feeling to be among so many old people. The only really old person he had ever known was his great-grandmother. But she lived in a city several hundred miles away, and the Dawsons didn't visit her often.

When Kit had time to look around, the room reminded him of his great-grandmother's apartment.

21

It had the same tidy but cluttered look. The warmth and the stuffiness were the same, too.

Little tables and cabinets and shelves were everywhere. Each was covered with vases and figurines. Under each useless object was a crocheted mat or a piece of painted tile. Crocheted or embroidered mats were on the arms and backs of all the chairs. The walls were crowded with pictures, mostly of people in out-of-date clothes.

After a few minutes Miss Rogers hobbled back. She carried a pitcher. Behind her came a tiny, withered old lady carrying a tray that held a glass and a plateful of small cookies. Miss Rogers poured pale liquid into a glass and handed it to Kit. The other old lady set the cookies on the table beside him.

"Now!" Miss Rogers beamed. She took off the black shawl. Her white hair was in an untidy knot on top of her head. "Tell us why you came here."

Kit took a sip from the glass. It was lemonade, but weaker, sweeter, and warmer than Kit liked it. He took a bite of a cookie, which tasted dry and crumbly. All the old people were looking at him expectantly. There was nothing to do but explain why he had peered through their gate. He told the story as briefly as he could.

Some of the old people were rather deaf and had to have Kit's words shouted into their ears by their neighbors. Some who had heard but hadn't understood demanded explanations. At last the discussions died away, and they all turned to stare at Kit.

"When I was a boy," one old man said sternly, "we made our own baseballs. Bats, too. Nobody ever heard of spending money on gloves."

"We were lucky to find time for a game," said another, "after we walked four miles to school and back, then chopped wood and carried in water. We also milked cows, fed the stock, and cleaned the barn."

"You were lucky!" This was the withered-up old lady. "I had the care of eight children and the house after my mother died. No play at all for me."

"No wonder the world's in the state it's in," pronounced Mr. McIntyre. "All children are spoiled today!"

The old men and old ladies nodded grimly. Plainly they thought Kit very spoiled and his story a shocking one. But at least there was no more talk of calling the police.

Kit got to his feet. "I'm sorry I bothered you," he said. "Thank you for the refreshments. Good night."

Mr. Benjamin walked with Kit to the gate, opened it to let him out, and closed it. As he walked away, Kit could hear a soft, clucking noise of puzzlement and disapproval. The gently wheezing voice of the old man said, "These young people! Expect the world, they do, handed to them on a plate."

Chapter 4

No Fooling, Kit!

"YOU'RE LATE, KIT!" Dinner was on the table, and Kit's father had an impatient eye on the clock.

"I'm sorry, Dad." Kit dropped his books on the hall table, propped his bat against the wall with his glove on the floor beside it, shucked off his jacket, and collapsed into his chair.

"You forgot to wash your hands, Kit," Mrs. Dawson said.

Kit dashed for the bathroom, splashed his hands with water, dabbed them with a towel, and dashed back again.

"I don't know how you manage to fritter away so much time," Kit's mother lamented. Mrs. Dawson went to a lot of trouble cooking for Kit and his father. Tonight she had baked something in pretty little blue-and-white dishes. There was a bright centerpiece of daffodils. Kit knew she must be disappointed that he had rushed in without even taking time to look.

"I'm sorry, Mother," he said.

"Kit's still looking for that Little League field, I suppose," his father said. "Might as well give up, Kit."

"I guess so," Kit sighed. Luckily neither of them asked just where he had been.

Kit's visit to the Elnathan F. Marley Home was the first event of his life that he kept absolutely to himself. In fact, he tried hard to forget the whole thing. It was too embarrassing to think about.

It was bad enough that he had been so scared. It was even worse that he had listened to all the mean things those old people had said about the kids of Millbrook without saying a word in defense of his friends.

Now he could think of all the things he should have said. He and his friends had tried to find their own place to play, but there wasn't one. He and his friends would have been perfectly willing to carry in wood and water. But why should they when it wasn't necessary? He couldn't very well walk four miles to school when the school was only four blocks from his house.

Kit knew just how he should have said those things—politely and reasonably so that not even the most disagreeable old person could have accused him of being rude. But, when he had the chance, he hadn't spoken at all. How could he have been so stupid?

After that night Kit and everybody else gave up looking for a place for a Little League field. Every street had been explored. The boys were convinced at last that there was no place to be had.

Boys of eleven or younger still talked hopefully of next season. Old-timers like Kit and Tom and Tony just tried to forget Little League. For them it was over. They stopped wishing and hoping.

But nobody could be gloomy all the time. April Fool's Day exploded with pranks and practical jokes. Kit arrived home from school earlier than usual, his mouth still burning from a piece of gum. Somebody had doctored it with tabasco sauce and had slyly substituted it for one of the sticks in his package.

In spite of his sore mouth, he was smiling. He could still see Tony's face when he opened the bag filled with dog biscuits which Kit had slipped into the place of an identical bag containing Tony's lunch. He had put over a good one on Tom, too, by opening the rings of Tom's notebook. When Tom stood up to read a report to the class, the pages fell out and scattered all over the room.

As Kit entered the house he could hear the telephone ringing. A moment later his mother called, "It's for you, Kit."

The voice was Tom's. It sounded very excited. "Hey, Kit! Guess what?"

Kit groaned. "You broke a leg and they had to shoot you."

"Oh, cut it out! I'm serious. You'd never guess in a million years, anyway. Kit, we've got a Little League field."

"Ha, ha, very funny," Kit said. "Listen, Tom, you've tried all day to fool me and you couldn't. What makes you think I'd fall for anything that corny?"

"But I'm not fooling, Kit! Just look in today's paper." Tom was putting on a good act, Kit thought. But he wasn't going to fall.

"Sure, Tom," he said. "And Willie Mays was sent to the minors. And your grandmother just left in a rocket for the moon."

"Okay, wise guy, you'll see." Tom slammed down the receiver so hard it hurt Kit's ear.

"Hey, Mom!" Kit called, when his ears had stopped ringing. "Where's today's paper?"

"In the mail box, I imagine."

Kit walked to the mail box slowly, wondering if Tom or some other pal was watching. He tucked the paper under his arm and strolled back to the house.

Once in the house, he hurried to unfold the newspaper. And there it was, right on the front page! MILLBROOK TO HAVE LITTLE LEAGUE FIELD, the headline said in big, black letters. Underneath, in smaller letters, USE OF MARLEY PROPERTY GRANTED FOR SEASON.

The Marley property? That must be the place where he had met all those old people. He settled down to read the story.

> Officials of the Millbrook Little League today announced that permission has been granted by the Board of Directors of the Elnathan F. Marley Home for the Aged for use of a portion of its grounds as a Little League playing field for the coming season.
>
> Use of the field is granted on condition that the property be restored to its former state at the end of the season and that players and spectators conduct themselves so as to avoid any disturbance to the residents.
>
> The Elnathan F. Marley Home, founded in 1901 under provisions in the will of the late Mr. Marley . . .

Kit didn't bother reading the rest of the story which went on for two whole columns. With a whoop of delight he dropped the paper and dashed for the telephone. He would give Tom the satisfaction of an apology for doubting his word. Then they could start planning for the season ahead.

But he pulled up short as his mother called, "What's all the excitement, Kit?" He picked up the paper and pointed out the headline.

"Why, that's wonderful news, Kit." His mother sat down and started to read the article. But somehow she didn't seem as surprised as Kit had expected her to be.

Then he remembered about his father's being on the Little League Board of Directors. Of course! This must be something that they had been working on all along. They had been keeping it a secret until everything was arranged. If only they had let the kids in on it, it would have saved Kit and his friends a lot of worry and unhappiness.

Those old people, too, must have known all about it. Yet they had made Kit tell the whole story to them again. They might have been told to keep it a secret, of course. Somehow the thought that he had been so earnest with them made him feel foolish.

Still, none of this mattered. The important thing was that the Little League had a field. There wouldn't be much time for tryouts or practice, but he and Tom and Tony wouldn't lose their twelve-year-old season. It was going to be a glorious summer after all.

Chapter 5

Mr. Ginger Takes Charge

THE MILLBROOK LITTLE LEAGUE sprang to life and worked feverishly to make up for lost time. Officials drew up schedules and ordered equipment and uniforms. Other officials arranged for tryouts, for working parties to get the new field in shape, for the use of the school fields for practice. Still others looked for new coaches and managers to replace men who had retired or moved away.

Everywhere in Millbrook gloves were being oiled. Bats were being sandpapered and their handles painstakingly taped. Little League shoes were being tried on, found to be outgrown, and hurriedly replaced. Team caps appeared like spring flowers bursting into many-colored bloom. The Colts' cap was gray with a purple brim.

In back yards, in vacant lots, and in corners of the school yard, sites for private practice were discovered where before they hadn't seemed to exist. Everywhere pitchers cautiously conditioned their arms and experimented with new pitches. Catchers did knee-bends to limber up unused muscles. Batters diligently practiced their swings.

Kit, Tom, and Tony arrived at the first practice with feelings wavering between hope and dread. The Colts would have a new manager this year, for their old one had moved away at the end of the previous season.

For a team like the Colts, it was terribly important to have a good manager. The Tigers, coming off a first-place season, would be swept along by their self-confidence. The Wildcats had enough talent to survive poor management. But the Colts needed someone who could make the most of ordinary material. They needed a man who could lift their spirits and make them feel like winners.

All the Colts were at practice ahead of time. They sprawled on benches or tossed baseballs back and forth. But the new manager was nowhere to be seen.

As Kit looked at his twelve-year-old teammates, he found himself feeling a little sorry for that unknown new manager. The Colts were an unpromising bunch. Bill Hobson, the only pitcher left from last season, was a solemn, awkward, slow-moving boy. Ted Erhart was a tow-headed scatterbrain. Bruce Rochester was a showoff. Though Kit hated to think it of one of his best friends, Tom Fairbanks was both a scatterbrain *and* a showoff. Tony Sheldon was a good kid who always tried hard, but he was fat and slow. As for himself, Kit Dawson hadn't exactly won any trophies.

The eleven-year-olds were even worse. Mike Parsons was another fatty. Web Redding was silent and shy, seeming almost afraid to move for fear of making a mistake. Ralph DeForest was so frail and wispy that he looked as if catching a hard-hit ball would knock him flat. Sam Holland and Martin Woolsey were new boys in town.

As for the ten-year-olds, no one could expect much of them. They were Bob Cutler, Lew Kingsley, Dave Scott, and Pete Harrison. Bob was the only one who handled a ball and glove as if he knew what to do with them.

At last the boys began to get bored and impatient. They started to chatter and laugh among themselves, to punch each other playfully, and to begin some impromptu wrestling matches.

Then there was a squeal of brakes, a crunch of gravel, and the whine of an engine. A small white convertible that looked like a bathtub on wheels whizzed down the drive and skidded to an abrupt halt.

Instantly the Colts became silent. They watched wide-eyed as a wiry little man with bright red hair, blue eyes, and a broad smile that showed gleaming white teeth, leaped out and dashed across the field.

"Well, boys!" the red-haired man cried jovially. "I'm your manager, Mr. Ginger. We haven't long to make ourselves a team, so let's not waste time. You, you, you, and you help me with the equipment." He stabbed a decisive finger at each of the four biggest boys. Kit was one of them.

In hardly any time at all, Mr. Ginger had a team positioned around the field with the left-overs assigned to play the part of baserunners. Then he started hitting out grounders, fly balls, and line drives in all directions. Every few minutes Mr. Ginger called someone in from his place and sent him to another position. Kit started practice in center field, came in to first base, and finally replaced Tony as catcher.

It was a bewildering sort of practice. Nobody stayed in one spot long enough to get used to it. Mr. Ginger shouted orders and advice incessantly, rushing the boys around until they were out of breath.

At last Mr. Ginger dropped his bat. Pulling out a handkerchief, he mopped his face. Then he said, "Whew! That was some workout! But, by George, we're going to have a team. It will be a real, driving, hustling, winning team, or my name's not Ed Ginger. Now, I want all of you in bed early at night. I want you to eat your meals and drink your milk. I want you to live like athletes, by George! And I

33

want you to hustle. Hustle all the time—on the field and off. I'll see you all Wednesday at the same time and at the same place. I want to see you ready to go—go—go!"

"Oh, brother!" Tony groaned as he dragged himself away from the field. "That guy's going to kill us!"

"Just what you need," Tom said heartlessly. "Work off some of that blubber."

Kit nodded happily. "Maybe Mr. Ginger really can make a winning team out of us. I'm going to do everything he says. And you guys better, if you know what's good for you."

Chapter 6

Kit Dawson, Catcher

No TEAM in the league practiced more often than the Colts. No team's practices moved faster or lasted longer. Mr. Ginger seemed to have unlimited time for his players, as well as an unlimited supply of energy and zeal. The Colts quickly caught the fire of his enthusiasm. They hustled and drove and tried with every ounce of energy they possessed.

Only one thing made Kit doubt Mr. Ginger's wisdom. That was his decision to make Kit the Colts' catcher. Of all the positions in baseball, catcher was the last one Kit had ever wanted.

Catching was a miserable job. A catcher was burdened with heavy, hot, and cumbersome equipment. Peering from behind his mask, all but hidden by his chest protector and shin guards, he resembled some monstrous beetle. Crouching behind the plate was almost unbearable torture. And to be confined to a dusty patch of ground behind home plate, with baseballs flying toward him and bats whizzing within inches of his head, made Kit feel that a catcher was to be pitied. He was sorry that he had let himself be trapped into such a lowly and dangerous job.

One of Kit's consolations for being of a light and wiry build was that he thought he would never be picked for a catcher. Catchers usually were solid and stocky.

But now the disaster had come. Mr. Ginger had made it clear without actually putting it into words. If Kit expected to be a regular player with the Colts, catching was what he would have to do. And Kit, reluctantly but with determination, had resolved to try.

The first few practices were pure torture. Kit sweated under the burden of mask and shin guards and chest protector. He couldn't help closing his eyes and shrinking from the ball as it sped toward him or ducking his head away from the wilder swings of the bat. At nights his muscles ached so that he could hardly sleep. Then, when he did drop off, he found himself reliving the miseries of practice in his dreams.

Little by little, the agony eased. Kit's muscles grew accustomed to their new movements and positions. After Mr. Ginger had shouted for perhaps the twentieth time, "Don't close your eyes, Kit! You've got to watch the ball all the way," Kit managed to keep himself from blinking. With open eyes, he discovered that the baseball flying toward him really wasn't so terrifying. It was his to control, and he no longer flinched from it.

His fear of the swinging bat took longer to overcome. Finally the day came when Kit simply didn't think about it any more. He also began to realize that the mask and shin guards and chest protector no longer felt cumbersome and heavy. They had become like parts of himself. When he took them off, he felt as if he were light and unprotected, as a beetle might feel without its shell.

Then something wonderful happened. Once his discomfort and fears were gone, Kit realized that he was the only player who could see everything that happened on the field. Pitcher, infielders, outfielders, baserunners—everyone was in front of him. He could see their every move and even their expressions. In a game, he thought excitedly, he could probably tell what each one planned to do. The looks of sudden doubt or determination would show in their faces. Kit wondered how he had ever endured long innings in the outfield with nothing to do but wait for a ball to be hit his way. Behind the plate there was action and excitement every minute. Now that he had tried it, Kit knew that this was the one place he wanted to be.

"By George, Kit! You're really going to make a catcher," Mr. Ginger shouted joyfully. Coming at just the time when Kit had decided he liked catching more than anything, the words completed his happiness.

Mr. Ginger showed Kit how to move for the ball with his whole body instead of just reaching out with his glove. He demonstrated how to lob the ball back to the pitcher in order to make it easy for him to receive. He showed how to throw low and straight to the bases so that the ball could be quickly used to tag a runner coming in. He taught Kit to cover the areas along the baselines in case of bad throws or bungled catches. He showed how to make signals that were easily visible to the pitcher and hard to detect by the opposition.

Kit worked hard and learned quickly. Day by day, he grew more at ease in his new position. And the more he learned, the more he became convinced of the importance of the job.

Mr. Ginger didn't work with Kit alone. He gave much attention to his young pitchers—Bob Cutler, Lew Kingsley, and Dave Scott, as well as the more experienced Bill Hobson. He had time for all the other players, too. There was Tom, settling down confidently at first. Ted Erhart seemed set to start at second base, with Ralph DeForest at third and Sam Holland at short. Tony had taken over center field, flanked by Web Redding and Bruce Rochester.

That seemed to be the starting lineup. However, all of them were encouraged to learn the fundamentals of other positions. Also, Mr. Ginger didn't neglect the boys who weren't on the lineup. He announced that there would be no bench-sitters on his team. Everyone would get a fair chance to play. The boys who weren't slated for regular positions got as much of Mr. Ginger's training and advice as those who were.

Kit wished that when he was ten he could have had the same sort of manager. He was glad to see that the younger boys were being prepared to step into infield or outfield positions. However, he felt sure that none of them would have an opportunity to stand behind the plate this year.

The shock was grave when, at the next-to-last practice, Mr. Ginger called to Kit as he was strapping on his shin guards. "You can rest a while, Kit. Web, let's see how you shape up as a catcher." Evidently Mr. Ginger didn't even mean to tell Kit how he had failed. And Kit had thought that he was developing into a pretty good catcher. Could he have been so bad that Mr. Ginger had decided to give up on him? Surely he didn't think that awkward, bashful Web Redding would make a better catcher?

Web looked downcast and half paralyzed with fear. Kit watched him put one shin guard on the wrong leg, fumble for a moment with the buckles, and then hastily take it off. A couple of young boys laughed, and Web's face turned bright red.

"Here, let me show you." Disappointed and angry as Kit was, he couldn't let Web go on suffering. After the equipment was on, Kit adjusted the straps to fit Web's smaller frame. "Don't get shook up," he said encouragingly. "It's not so tough."

Standing back to watch Web receive the first few pitches, Kit couldn't suppress a smile of grim satisfaction. Web looked scared to death and hopelessly clumsy. Maybe that would show Mr. Ginger that Kit Dawson wasn't so easy to replace!

Mr. Ginger sauntered over to stand beside Kit. "Looks pretty bad, doesn't he? But if we can't make a second-string catcher out of Web, I don't know where we'll find one."

Giddy with relief, Kit demanded, "Aw, what do we need one for, Mr. Ginger?"

Mr. Ginger looked surprised. "Suppose you came down with the measles?"

"I've had the measles," Kit said smugly.

"Then what about next year?"

Kit knew Mr. Ginger had a point. Every manager tried to build for next season and that meant training replacements for his twelve-year-olds. Studying Web more sympathetically, Kit said, "He does look pretty feeble. But I guess everyone looks that way at first. I'll try to put in some extra practice with him."

"Thanks, Kit." Mr. Ginger gave him a friendly pat on the shoulder. "I'd appreciate that."

Chapter 7

Quiet, Like Little Mice

THE LAST PRACTICE before opening day was always
a special occasion. Not only was it the last chance to
bolster up weaknesses in the team, but there were
other important things to take care of. What the
players looked forward to most was getting their
uniforms.

A uniform turned an ordinary boy into a real
baseball player. Practice was fun, but it was not
much different from the games played at school or
in vacant lots. But a planned game was important
enough to be watched by parents and friends, even
by strangers sometimes. Games were reported in the
Journal, side by side with accounts of fires and traffic
accidents and meetings of the town council. And yet
in the minds of the boys just one thing transformed
a pastime into an event. It wasn't the opening-day
parade or the throwing out of the first ball of the

season that made the difference. It was that moment at final practice when the uniforms were handed out.

Even such an important ceremony couldn't be completely without humor. When cocky little Bob Cutler was handed uniform number four, he looked startled and then furious. The rest of the Colts roared with laughter.

"Guess that'll put you in your place," Tom gasped, when he could control his giggles. The uniforms were numbered in order, growing larger as the numbers increased, and everyone knew Bob considered himself big enough for double numbers, even though he was only ten.

Skinny Ralph DeForest drew number seven. That had been Kit's uniform the year before.

"You can get your brother in there with you, Ralphie," Kit said. Last spring his mother had taken two enormous tucks in the waist of the pants, but they still had fit like a tent.

There were groans of mock-sympathy when Bill Hobson held up his uniform, number twelve. "Boy!" Ted Erhart cried. "Let's take up a collection to retire that suit." Number twelve was threadbare and faded. The pants were patched on the seat and at the knees. The shirt had a patch at one shoulder and another halfway down the back.

"I'll be afraid to let go a pitch, Mr. Ginger," Bill said mournfully. "I'm scared this thing will fall apart and leave me standing in my underwear."

Mr. Ginger tried to look stern, but he was struggling against laughter. "Then be sure to put on your best underwear before a game," he advised.

Kit threw Bill a mocking grin when he saw that his own uniform looked brand-new. Then Kit nearly dropped the uniform which was still neatly encased by a plastic bag. He suddenly realized that he had been given number thirteen.

Last season's number thirteen, Ricky Taber, had hardly ever left the bench, Kit remembered. The year before that the boy who had worn number thirteen had broken an ankle sliding into second. No, there wasn't a doubt in Kit's mind that bad luck went with that number. But what could he do? To complain to Mr. Ginger wouldn't do any good. He would just laugh and say that it was silly to be superstitious. And the other kids would think he was trying to shove his bad luck onto somebody else. So Kit decided to suffer whatever misfortune was coming and hope that it wouldn't be too bad.

When the uniforms had been distributed, everybody expected to be dismissed after a few words about when and where to assemble for opening day. But Mr. Ginger solemnly said, "Sit down, boys. I have something important to tell you."

When everyone was seated Mr. Ginger went on. "As you know, we're lucky to have a playing field this season. We only have one because the people at the Marley Home for the Aged gave us permission to use part of their grounds. I hope you're all grateful to them."

All the Colts nodded emphatically. "Yes, sir!" they chorused.

"Part of the agreement," Mr. Ginger then said, "was that their permission might be withdrawn at any time if the property were damaged or if we disturbed them." Mr. Ginger took a deep breath and looked more solemn than ever. "The people at the Home are very old. Nobody under seventy is allowed to live there. And older people—well, they're not used to boys. Things will disturb them that might not bother your parents or the other people you know."

The Colts nodded dutifully, but they were beginning to give each other doubtful looks.

Mr. Ginger took a paper from his pocket and began to read from it. "All members of the Millbrook Little League are to observe the following rules while using the playing field adjacent to the Marley Home for the Aged:

"One: Entrance to the field will be only by the main gate located on Marley Place.

"Two: Approach to the playing area will be only by way of the gravel path at the edge of the grounds. Walking on the grass, except for the playing field itself, is forbidden.

"Three: There must be no littering of the grounds or field.

"Four: There will be no shouting or other loud noises, either from players or from spectators."

The Colts had nodded in meek agreement as Mr. Ginger read the first three rules. But at the fourth there was a chorus of protest.

"Mr. Ginger! How can we play ball without yelling?"

"You mean nobody can cheer? Even if somebody hits a home run?"

"I can just see my dad watching a game without opening his mouth!"

"Or my mother! Looks like this'll be the shortest season on record," someone mourned.

Mr. Ginger held up both hands for silence. "A letter has been mailed to all parents and to everyone else we think might want to attend the games. It explains the rules and our reasons for making them. I'm sure your parents and friends are as anxious as you to go on using this field. I'm sure they'll all cooperate. So if each one of you keeps the rules, there'll be nothing to worry about. Do you all agree to do your best to abide by them?"

"Yes, sir." The voices were subdued. The Colts left the field slowly with bowed heads and dragging feet.

"Great fun it's going to be," Kit grumbled when he, Tom, and Tony turned toward home. "Can't you see us running the bases on our tippy-toes and being quiet like little mice?"

"Yeah," Tony agreed. "Some fun."

Tom sighed. "It won't be easy to live up to all those rules."

"No, it won't," Kit said dejectedly. "But they are doing us a big favor, so I guess we'll have to try."

As Kit walked home, he thought about all those rules; and then he remembered the number of his uniform. There might be a worse way to start his twelve-year-old season, Kit thought, but he couldn't imagine what it would be.

Chapter 8

Kit Keeps a Promise

"GOOD MORNING," Kit's mother said to him when he came down to breakfast on Saturday. "Isn't this a perfect opening day?"

"Yes'm. It sure is." His parents looked so happy that Kit forced himself to smile.

Kit's father chuckled happily as he stirred his coffee. "Just wait until you see that field! You haven't seen it yet, have you?"

"No, sir. Mr. Ginger said if any of us were caught hanging around there, we'd be off the team before we knew what hit us."

"Good!" Mr. Dawson said. "I'm glad the managers are getting the message across. All we need is one boy making a nuisance of himself, and we might lose the field before we even have a chance to use it."

When Kit changed into his uniform, it fit so perfectly and looked so well that he almost forgot about his unlucky number. He met Tom and Tony at the corner, and they strolled toward the square.

"We'll beat the ears off those Stags," Tom predicted, "and start the season right."

"Hope so," Tony said. "They were pretty tough last season, though."

"Only when Bob Wayne was pitching, and he's not around this year," Kit said. "We don't have a thing to worry about."

The talking died away. Kit was repeating to himself all the things Mr. Ginger had told him, hoping he would remember everything and not make any mistakes. With Bill on the mound there wouldn't be too much to worry about. Bill had been a starting pitcher all last season and could be counted on to keep the situation under control. And of course Bill would pitch since he was the only member of the Colts with pitching experience.

Glancing at Tom and Tony, Kit knew that they too were rehearsing Mr. Ginger's instructions. Like himself, they would be starting in positions new to them. They probably were depending a good deal on Bill's pitching, too.

The parade moved down Main Street to the loud music of the Fire Department band and the cheers of the crowd. Passing the corner that led to the old field, some of the boys glanced wistfully in that

48

direction. The old field had been a pleasant place where kids could flock from any direction, hang around even when there was no game, and make as much noise as they pleased. Now a clutter of machinery, piles of lumber and cement block, and the beginnings of an ugly metal skeleton made it a hopeless ruin. The players grew quiet, their smiles fading. Kit was sure they wished their new field was anywhere else except in the back yard of an old people's home.

As the parade turned into Marley Place, the band stopped playing. Parents and friends stopped cheering. Footsteps seemed suddenly muffled, as if everyone were moving on tiptoe.

When the Colts' part of the parade came around the bend, Kit could see Mr. Benjamin standing in front of the big iron gates. Kit's father and another official of the Little League stepped forward, and the men shook hands and exchanged a few words. Then Mr. Benjamin unlocked the gates, and the two officials swung them open so that the parade could pass through.

As Mr. Dawson had said, the field was a beauty. It had been laid out so that the diamond was as far away as possible from the house. The outfield was bordered by one of those portable snow fences which can be put up and taken down easily.

Kit had never expected to hear "The Star-Spangled Banner" played like a lullaby. But today every instrument was at its lowest possible volume. And there was no real flag-raising, for a flag was already flying from the Home's flagpole.

There were some speeches Kit didn't listen to, and then it was announced that Mr. Benjamin would throw out the first ball. Kit stared. An old guy like that? Why, he was so bent and feeble he hardly looked able to walk to the pitcher's mound.

Once he reached the mound, the old man rubbed up the ball as if he knew what to do with it. He drew himself up, glared fiercely down at the president of the league who was acting as catcher, and whipped the ball straight across the plate. That done, he shrank back into his bent-over feebleness, shook hands once more with the officials, and hobbled off toward the house.

Everybody relaxed a bit. The field looked in fine shape, the ceremonies had gone off smoothly, and Kit began to hope that nothing bad would happen that day.

"All right, Kit. Get your gear on and start warming-up Bob," Mr. Ginger said briskly.

Kit's jaw dropped. "Bob? I thought Bill was going to pitch."

Mr. Ginger shook his head. "He took a spill off his bike yesterday and hurt his wrist. He'll be all right in the outfield, but he can't pitch. He should be ready for the next game, though."

Kit tried not to show how disheartened he felt,

and he could tell that the rest of the players were also concealing dismay. After all, it was no use making Bob's first start even more difficult by letting him know how much they wished Bill were pitching. Bob wasn't really too bad. He threw pretty hard for a ten-year-old, and most of the time he got the ball over the plate. Though he had never pitched in a real league game, he had been a hot-shot on last season's farm team. His confident smile and the cocky way he moved were proof that he expected the same success here.

Amid the silence of players and audience, Bob struck out the first batter. But the next one wiped the grin from his face by sending the first pitch over second base for a single. Bob scowled angrily as he toed the rubber. He wasn't taking time to think between pitches, and he certainly wasn't pacing himself to last out the game. Kit tried to signal him to slow down, but the pitch was already on its way. Bob had let it go too soon. Wildly out of control, the ball soared high and inside and thudded against the batter's safety helmet. Now there were two runners on base, only one man was out, and Bob looked desperately upset and confused. Kit called time.

He looked appealingly at Mr. Ginger, wishing that he would come out and talk to Bob. But Mr. Ginger didn't move, so Kit knew that it was up to him. He tried to remember what Mr. Ginger had said to him those times when he had practiced pitching. Then he tried to say the same things to Bob.

"You're doing great, Bob. You've got a lot on the ball. Just take your time. Let the batter wait till you get good and ready. Tell you what—let me set the pace for a while. Don't throw until you see me drop my hand like this."

Bob grinned sheepishly. "You're right, Kit. Having that kid hit my best pitch so easy got me rattled. But I'll be all right now."

Kit felt relieved at having been able to hear Bob's voice. He had been fighting a sensation that his hearing was suddenly gone. It was just the strangeness of playing ball in nearly complete silence.

The next batter sent a high fly to right field for the second out, but the runners had time to advance. Then the Stags' burly catcher belted a drive that bounced over the fence for a ground-ruled double, and both runners scored. Bob looked pale and shaken.

"Don't let it bother you, Bob. You're doing fine," Kit called.

But Bob, tight-lipped with determination, missed the plate with a three-and-two pitch to put the next runner on. Next Tony, lumbering across center field after a fly that should have meant the third out, let the ball glance off the edge of his outstretched glove. With the bases loaded, Kit called time again.

"I'm just no good." Bob sounded on the edge of

tears. "They hit everything I throw. Can't Mr. Ginger send in somebody else?"

Kit knew he had to talk fast and convincingly. "It's not your fault. You got a bad break. Just keep throwing the way you've been doing, and I guarantee we'll be all right. We'll get those runs back, and you can start a new ball game."

Luckily for Kit, the next fly ball was to the right; and fleet-footed Bruce gathered it in.

Bill led off for the Colts to start the new season. When Bill struck out, Kit's heart sank. He had promised Bob that they would get those runs back for him. If they didn't, Bob would have little reason to believe what he said from now on.

But then Bruce drew a walk, and that brought Bob to the plate with Kit next in line. Kit pulled on a helmet, swung a couple of bats vigorously, and called, "Just get on base, kid! Remember what I promised."

Bob grinned, let the first pitch go by for a strike, and sent the next through the hole for a single. Bruce raced all the way to third.

Now things were set up for Kit to keep his promise. But could he? Getting a hit now would make him a rock of dependability upon which the whole team could rely. Not getting one would make him— just nothing. He made up his mind that nothing hittable would get by him, so he swung at the first pitch. The bat met it, and he ran as hard as he could. A moment later he was safe on first. Bob was on second, and Bruce had crossed the plate with one of those runs he had promised.

Tom hit a grounder that the first baseman bobbled to load the bases. Then Ted Erhart's towering fly was caught in center field for the second out, but Bob had tagged up and scored the tying run. Even though Web struck out to end the inning, Kit's promise had been kept.

After that Bob settled down and pitched slowly and carefully. Though he gave up several more hits, he didn't get rattled again. The Colts took the lead and finally won by a score of thirteen to nine.

"Not what you'd call a pitcher's battle," Bob said ruefully when it was over.

"What's the difference, as long as we won?" Tom grinned. He was feeling good, for he had gotten two hits. He also made an error that had cost a run, but that didn't matter now.

"We're going to have a great season. Really great!" Kit proclaimed. The morning's fears were forgotten in his delight at the three hits he had garnered in this first game. "The only thing is, it gave me a funny feeling when things were so quiet. No matter what happened, all you could hear was that soft little bit of hand-clapping. If we had been at the old field, you'd have heard the yelling all over town when we tied the score."

Tony shrugged his big shoulders. He had no hits

to rejoice over and an error to worry about, so he didn't look as happy as the rest. "Well, we're not at the old field now, so we'd better watch it," he said. "Just remember not to play too well. That way people won't get excited. If anybody hits a home run—look out! Some guy will let out a yell, and we'll land outside on our ears."

Chapter 9

Mr. Ginger Sounds Off

THE COLTS' VICTORY in their first game convinced Kit that all his worries had been for nothing. The others seemed to share his feelings.

"I thought we were sunk when Bill couldn't pitch," Tom said, as he and Kit and Tony walked toward the field on the day of their second game. "But we've got some good hitters. We don't have to depend on just one pitcher."

"It'll be good to have Bill in there today, though," Kit said. "With him, it ought to be a breeze."

Tony didn't join the confident predictions. "I wouldn't be too sure," he said gloomily. "Those Tigers will be a lot tougher than the Stags. Bill's all right, but he's no ball of fire. His pitching isn't bad, but when it comes to fielding his position he's about as much help as a broken crutch. He can get rattled, too, when something goes wrong. And when Bill gets rattled, he doesn't snap out of it as fast as Bob."

"Then we've got to back him up and not give him anything to get nervous about," Kit said. After his success in settling down Bob in his first start, Kit felt ready to handle just about anything.

Compared with the excitement of opening day, things seemed very quiet. Players walked silently up Marley Place. They slipped through the gate and walked sedately along the path to the field. Managers and spectators parked their cars on Pleasant Avenue and also entered quietly. Even the umpires, when they arrived, did the same. Everyone behaved in a subdued, businesslike manner.

"I'm proud of you, boys," Mr. Ginger told the Colts as he called them in from their pregame warm-up and prepared to announce the lineup. "You see now that you can call to each other without yelling at the tops of your voices. Just keep up the good work. Those people in the home won't even know there's a game going on. Then they can't have anything to complain about."

Kit glanced toward the gloomy old house. With closed doors and blank windows, it was as quiet as a tomb. As the Tigers took the field and the umpires assumed their positions, not a single old man or old lady was in sight.

Bill started badly by grounding out. But Tom

and Bob drew successive bases on balls, and Tom scored on Kit's single. Two men on and only one out roused hopes of a big inning and also brought gentle applause and soft-voiced calls of encouragement from the bleachers. Then Ted popped to the third baseman for an inning-ending double play.

Still, one run could be a substantial lead with a good pitcher like Bill on the mound.

"Just remember," cautioned Mr. Ginger as the Colts got ready to take the field, "the first one who starts yelling his head off is going to be mighty sorry."

As he crouched behind the plate, Kit felt his confidence growing. There was plenty of zip in Bill's warm-up pitches, and his control seemed even better than usual. Almost every time he was able to put the ball exactly where Kit's signal called for it. Just to see Bill out there, twice as big as Bob and with sober confidence on his face instead of Bob's cocky grin, made Kit feel that the game was in the bag.

Bill's first pitch was a strike on the inside corner. His next was low and outside. The batter swung and missed. The next came waist-high right down the middle, a perfect pitch that no batter dared let go. But just before it reached the plate, it began to sink. The Tigers' shortstop hit the top of the ball and bounced it weakly toward second.

A good fielding pitcher would have grabbed the

ball for an easy out, but nobody expected that of Bill. Ted moved over and waited for it to bounce again. But the bounce wasn't exactly what Ted expected, for a pebble deflected the ball a bit to his right. When Ted lunged for it, the ball glanced off the edge of his glove and into the outfield.

"Er-HART!" Mr. Ginger's sudden, ear-shattering roar seemed to shake the whole field. He was on his feet, shaking his fist in the direction of second base. "How could you pull a bonehead trick like that, Ted? Let's wake *up* out there!"

Players, spectators, and even umpires stared at Mr. Ginger in horror. Mr. Ginger, more horrified than anyone else, dropped his arm to his side. His stricken face slowly reddened until it almost matched his hair.

From his position behind the plate, Kit was the only player who had the house directly in view. With a sinking heart, he saw a curtain at an upstairs window pulled back to reveal the pale glimmer of a face. But by the time everyone else turned to look apprehensively in that direction, the curtain had dropped again. A little sigh of relief swept around the field like a breath of wind.

Kit opened his mouth to tell what he had seen, then firmly closed it again. Soon enough Mr. Benjamin would come storming out to complain. Or perhaps it would be Miss Rogers charging like a vengeful witch with her flapping black shawl. Let the rest of them enjoy feeling safe for a few more minutes.

Behind Kit, the plate umpire cleared his throat. "Batter up!" he said in a pointedly gentle voice. The game went on.

The next batter sent the ball at Ted again, but this time it was on the ground. Ted, white-faced and over-anxious, got it firmly in his glove. But his throw was hard and too high. The ball soared over Bob's head as he raced to cover second. Now there were two runners on.

This time Mr. Ginger called softly, "Take it easy, Ted. Don't let it bother you." But Kit knew that the forced kindliness of his voice wasn't going to erase Ted's memory of Mr. Ginger's outburst a few minutes before. The tow-headed second base-man looked as if he had lost hope of ever doing anything right again.

To make things worse, Bill looked ready to explode with fury. And who could blame him? With decent support he would have had two out instead of two on. Throwing too quickly and too hard, he walked the Tigers' pitcher to load the bases.

Kit called time and trotted to the mound. But, as Tom had predicted, Bill wasn't as easy to soothe as Bob had been. With set jaw and gray eyes hard with rage, he snarled, "I've got to try for strikeouts. If anybody hits the ball, those clowns that are supposed to be fielding let it get away from them."

"Ted's having tough luck," Kit pleaded. "He'll settle down. Just put it over the plate, and give the rest of us a chance."

With great deliberation Bill put the next pitch over the middle of the plate. The Tigers' center fielder bounced the ball off the fence to drive in two runs.

So much for that bit of advice. Kit seemed to feel Bill's anger scorching him all the way from the mound. He called hopefully, "Don't let it worry you, kid." Bill scowled fiercely and went back to firing the ball too quickly and too hard. Another batter walked.

Just as Kit was resigning himself to the prospect of having the game called for darkness before a Tiger was out, Bill racked up two strikeouts in a row. Bill really hadn't improved much, but the kids near the end of the batting order were swinging at bad pitches.

Then came two more bases on balls and a run forced in. Mr. Ginger stopped his useless efforts at encouragement and sat silently. A gloomy quiet settled over players and spectators. Even the Tigers, though eager for victory, didn't enjoy getting runs this way.

The Tigers had batted around, and the little short-stop was up again. He hit the ball exactly as he had hit it his first time up, but this time Ted grabbed it firmly and threw it just right. Tom had it in his glove while the runner was yards away. The miserable inning was over.

"I said the first one to start yelling his head off would be mighty sorry," Mr. Ginger greeted his team as they came in. "And I am. I guess I've got a temper to match my hair, and sometimes it gets away from me. I hope if I ever say anything as mean as that again you'll know my hair got the best of my head and ignore it. Ted, that last play was just about perfect."

Ted responded with a shy, one-sided grin. He didn't smile often, for he was self-conscious about the braces on his teeth. "Thanks, Mr. Ginger," he said. "I deserved to be yelled at. And I guess nobody over there heard it."

"Lucky for me." Mr. Ginger pretended to shudder. "If they had, I probably would have been run out of town. Guess the old folks had their hearing aids turned off. I'll be extra careful from now on, and I know you'll be careful, too. Now, let's get Bill some runs. Give him a chance to pitch his kind of game. By George, we'll win this game yet."

Although Bill settled down to pitch five scoreless innings and Kit, Tom, and Tony each got one hit, the Colts never did catch up. The Tigers hung on to win, four to three.

Still, the Colts weren't downhearted. In fact, their confidence increased when they had time to take stock of their performance.

"Throw out that first bad inning, and we'd have slaughtered them," Tom crowed.

Everyone agreed. That first inning was something to forget. Nothing like it, including Mr. Ginger's noisy outburst, could ever happen again. As for that mighty yell which everyone except Kit thought had gone unheard, each boy went home thankful that he hadn't been the one to turn it loose.

Chapter 10

A Figure of Doom

"I THINK YOU BOYS deserve medals for the way you've behaved." Mrs. Dawson smiled at Kit across the dinner table. "It's not easy to be quiet when you're having fun. And to think that every boy on every team has kept it up for a whole week! By this time it's probably a habit."

Kit grinned broadly. "The kids got a laugh when a manager was the first one to slip. Poor Mr. Ginger! I thought he'd die when he realized what he'd done."

"I hope it didn't make the boys lose respect for him." Mr. Dawson frowned.

"Oh, no!" Kit was astonished at the idea. "It would have, maybe, if he hadn't said right away how sorry he was. We don't expect grownups to be perfect. But we do get mad when they try to make us think they are. If he'd told us that it was all right for him to shout but that he'd better not hear a peep out of us, we'd probably hate him."

"Hmm. I see what you mean."

It was amazing how quickly habits could change. In just a week Little League baseball in Millbrook had been transformed from a thoughtlessly noisy pastime to a carefully quiet one.

Even when Kit smashed out a long double in the third inning to send Bob and Tom across the plate and give the Colts a three-to-one lead in their third game, there was no real cheering. There was only a polite spattering of applause, a few low-voiced cries of congratulation, and scattered groans from Wildcat sympathizers.

"By George, this is great!" Mr. Ginger said happily. "What did I tell you? Those old folks won't even know we're here. Just keep up the good work."

Kit didn't have a worry in the world as he slipped into his catcher's gear. The Colts were playing heads-up baseball. He had two hits in his two times at bat. Bill was pitching at top form with four strikeouts in two innings. And with it all, every player as well as every spectator was a model of quiet and good behavior. If the people in the Home were all taking afternoon naps, no noise from the field would disturb them.

When Bill wafted one of his best pitches across

the outside corner, the batter swung and missed by a mile. Kit tossed the ball back and then glanced automatically toward the house. His jaw dropped, and a look of consternation came over his face.

Bill saw the look and turned to see what had caused it. Others quickly followed his example until everyone was staring toward the house.

Walking toward them across the grass was Mr. Benjamin. Even though he was still some distance away, it was easy to see that his brows were drawn together in a scowl and that his lips were pressed into a sternly unsmiling line.

First to recover from the strange paralysis which had seized everyone was the plate umpire. He stepped briskly from behind Kit, pulled a whisk broom from his pocket, and brushed off home plate. "Play ball," he said, softly.

Bill glanced over his shoulder at the grim-faced Mr. Benjamin, still far away but approaching steadily like a figure of doom. Then he turned to face the batter. Plainly he was making a great effort to pull himself together, and just as plainly it wasn't working. His pitch bounced on the plate, and the next one went into the dirt. The next two soared over the batter's head.

Kit was too distracted to think of calling for time out. All he could do was try to keep his eyes off Mr. Benjamin's slowly advancing figure long enough to catch Bill's wild throws.

Bill, desperately trying to settle down, started aiming with great deliberation at the plate. The Wildcats were also nervous, but not nervous enough to let such an opportunity pass. They responded with three successive hits, two of them doubles, before Bob broke the spell by pulling in a high fly for the first out. Bill perked up enough to get a strikeout, but he allowed another run-producing hit before he fanned the Wildcats' right fielder to end the inning.

All this while Mr. Benjamin had been approaching at a snail's pace. As the Colts came in and the Wildcats took the field, he finally arrived at the edge of the diamond. But he approached none of the players or officials. Neither did he join the crowd of spectators in the bleachers. He just stood with his hands clasped behind his back and a grim look on his face.

"Guess he'll let us finish the game before he says anything," Kit muttered to Tom, as Tom picked up a bat to lead off. "Come on. Knock one out of here. Show him we aren't as bad as we looked just now."

Tom shook his head despairingly. "If they're going to kick us off the field and we can't play any more, what difference does it make? But I can't figure out what we did. Everybody's been so careful."

Kit shrugged, trying to look as if he didn't care. "Who knows? Maybe somebody dropped a gum wrapper on the grass."

"We might as well give up," Tom groaned. He drooped to the plate, grounded weakly to first, and walked back to slump on the bench.

Kit wasn't going to give up so easily. Suppose this was the Colts' last game? The thing to do was to go down fighting. He waited for a good pitch, drove it hard past the shortstop, and was safe at first. When Web sent a weak grounder toward the mound, Kit was off fast and slid into second. But Web, showing no more spirit than Tom, was out. Next Bruce bounced the ball feebly toward third, and Kit was safe by a mile. But Bruce ran half-heartedly for first and was out to end the inning.

Kit walked toward the Colts' bench with clenched fists, boiling inside. What a bunch of quitters! He'd like to grab the whole team and shake some sense into them.

He looked up, and found himself scowling straight into Mr. Benjamin's eyes. The gray eyes were surprisingly shrewd for such a very old man. Mr. Benjamin looked straight back at him and then, to Kit's surprise, slowly shook his head.

That did it! Kit told himself as he hurried into his catcher's equipment. The old man must have thought that he was silently begging him to change his mind and let them keep on using the field. By shaking his head, he'd been replying that it was no use.

Well, he'd show Mr. Benjamin! Even if it was

the last game that the old people allowed them to play, he'd prove to Mr. Benjamin that he couldn't scare Kit Dawson the way he had the rest of the Colts.

But it was hard to prove anything, the way the rest of the Colts were playing. Bill couldn't keep his mind on pitching, and the Wildcat batters took advantage of every mistake. They slammed out hits as if at batting practice, while the disheartened Colts went down in order.

Kit, aching to prove that at least one player on his team had some fight left, didn't get another chance at bat. Tom went down swinging at a bad pitch for the final out, and the Wildcats had a nine-to-three victory.

Now Mr. Benjamin would speak to the managers, and that would wind up the shortest Little League season on record, thought Kit glumly. He started gathering up bats and helmets and putting them into the equipment bag. He didn't want to look. But after a moment he couldn't help turning. All he saw was the two managers talking fast with their heads close together. Mr. Benjamin wasn't with them.

Kit's eyes searched the bleachers and then along the edges of the field. Finally he looked toward the house. The bent-over figure in shabby black clothes and broad-brimmed black hat was making its way slowly back.

Kit waited until the two managers stopped talking

and then pounced on Mr. Ginger. "Why are they throwing us out, Mr. Ginger? What did we do?"

Mr. Ginger shook his head, looking as puzzled as Kit felt. "I don't know, Kit. Nobody seems to know. I thought that when the game was over Mr. Benjamin would tell us we were through. But he never said a word. He just stood there watching, shaking his head once in a while and looking mad and disgusted. But then he just walked away. I can't figure it out."

Kit sighed. "Maybe he decided to call the president of the League or write a letter. He sure ruined our day. We were winning until he showed up."

Mr. Ginger nodded sadly. "That's right. I suppose I should have said something to cheer you boys up, but it didn't seem any use. The Wildcats weren't playing good baseball either. They just didn't fall apart as badly as the Colts did. Kit, how did you keep from going to pieces with the rest of the team?"

Kit grinned sheepishly. He was pleased that Mr. Ginger had noticed how hard he had tried. "I guess the way he looked at us made me mad. I just wanted to show him."

"Show him what, Kit?"

Kit shrugged and shook his head. If he had said that he wanted to prove that Millbrook boys weren't really as soft and lazy and spoiled as Mr. Benjamin and the rest of the people at the Marley Home thought, he would have had to tell Mr. Ginger what had been said that day weeks ago. And that would have led to explaining how he had blundered into their Home and maybe even letting Mr. Ginger guess how scared he had been.

That was the last thing Kit wanted to talk about, for he still burned with shame every time he remembered it.

Chapter II

Jinxed Again

THE COLTS APPROACHED the field for their next game feeling like intruders. When they had left it after their disgraceful defeat by the Wildcats, they hadn't expected to return. But no word had come that the game had been canceled, so Thursday afternoon they assembled for their game with the Bears.

"I suppose we'll just get started, and somebody'll come out and chase us," Tom grumbled. "What's going to happen, Kit?"

Everyone expected Kit to know what was going on because his father was a League officer. Sometimes his father did give him bits of information to pass along, but this time Kit knew that his father was as much in the dark as anyone.

"Who knows?" Kit said. "Maybe they decided to give us another chance. All we can do is go ahead and play until someone tells us we can't." He raised his voice to include all the other Colts standing around. "And for Pete's sake, let's get in there and play ball. If those people decide to throw us out, there's nothing we can do. But we don't have to let them scare us into looking like a bunch of clowns."

"That's right."

"Sure, Kit. We'll give it all we've got this time."

"We'll slaughter them."

The Colts looked fiercely determined. They'd show the Bears that the Colts could bounce back and look better than ever.

The Bears exuded confidence as they warmed up. But the Colts only stood around wondering what had happened to Mr. Ginger. Starting time was getting close, and without a manager the Colts wouldn't be allowed to play. Though nobody believed Mr. Ginger would let the team down by failing to appear, it was hard not to feel uneasy.

"Think he could've had an accident?" Dave Scott, the baby of the team, asked timidly.

The older boys jeered at the idea. But as the minutes passed their solemn faces showed that they were beginning to think about it.

Kit knew he should be getting a pitcher warmed up, but he didn't know which one. Bill had already pitched his allowed innings for the week. Bob, like Mr. Ginger, was missing. The others that Mr. Ginger had considered as possible starters were Lew Kingsley, Pete Harrison, and Dave. As far as Kit could see, there was little to choose among them. They were all pretty bad. Just to be doing something, he got on his gear and lined up the three. They started tossing the ball around to get their arms limbered up.

The umpires arrived, and the Colts' feeble hopes died. Forfeiting a game was the worst thing that could happen—even worse than the humiliating collapse they had suffered last time.

In desperation Kit shed his catcher's gear and told Tom that he would be right back. Then he raced down the gravel path and out the gate. He almost collapsed with relief when he saw Mr. Ginger hurrying along Marley Place, struggling with two heavy duffel bags full of equipment.

Kit shouldered one of the bags. "Boy, am I glad to see you, Mr. Ginger," he cried. "The umps are already here."

With his free hand Mr. Ginger reached a handkerchief and wiped the perspiration from his forehead. "Sorry I'm late," he gasped. "What a time I've had! I'd promised to give Bob a ride. When I stopped for him, he looked kind of droopy and didn't have much to say. I guess I didn't want to notice, because I was planning to have him pitch. I was busy telling him to take his time, to keep his pitches low, and so on. Then I happened to look at him when the sun was shining right in his face. He had his eyes squinched up, and there were little red bumps all over his face. So I took him to Dr. Long's office. All he needed was one look. Measles! So I had to drive Bob home and explain to his mother."

"I started warming up Lew and Pete and Dave, since Bob wasn't there," Kit said. "I figured you might want to start one of them, but I didn't know which."

"Kit," Mr. Ginger said, "I can't go with any of those three. They're just not ready. It'll have to be you."

"Me?" Kit yelped. He almost dropped the duffel bag in his astonishment. "I'm no pitcher, Mr. Ginger."

"You'll have to be. You've got a strong arm, and you've had plenty of playing experience even if you haven't pitched before. You're the only one who can give us a chance."

"Who'll catch, then?"

"I think that Web can handle it."

For the first time Kit was happy to have his team playing the visitors' role. It postponed the awful moment when he would have to take the mound. Fortunately, the opposing pitcher didn't seem particularly strong. He loaded the bases with walks before he got the final out, and that made Kit feel a little more hopeful.

On the mound, Kit had to hold himself stiff to

keep from shaking all over. If he hadn't kept his jaws clenched tight, his teeth would have chattered. He tried to keep his eyes on Web and his mind on the batter. He tried to forget the hundreds of staring eyes watching him. But he couldn't.

His warm-up pitches at least stayed within Web's reach, and that was something. Then the first batter stepped up. Kit tried to remember what sort of hitter the Bears' first baseman was so that he could figure out how he should pitch to him. But his brain seemed paralyzed, his mind a perfect blank. Web had two fingers pointed downward. Kit had given that signal dozens of times, but now he couldn't think what it meant.

Kit fixed his mind on just one idea. It was a piece of advice he had handed out freely when others were pitching, and now it was the only thing he could remember. Don't give them walks. Get the ball over the plate.

His advice to others had sounded easy to follow. But when he tried it himself, he felt the ball slip too quickly from his shaking hand. It veered wildly to his left, went behind the batter, and in passing brushed the seat of his pants. The boy laughed as he dropped his bat and trotted to first base.

Kit took lots of time before he tried again. He pretended to tie his shoe, scuffed up some dirt around the mound, and shook off Web's first signal even though he had no idea what it meant. All the time he was taking deep breaths and trying desperately to get his brain back into working order. He remembered how Mr. Ginger had taught them to count "One, two, three," in the pitching drills. "One—weight forward on the right foot to get set. Two—weight back on the left foot for the windup. Three—weight forward, step and throw!" This time he counted, just the same way.

The batter lifted a high fly over the infield. Kit couldn't trust anyone else to get it and almost collided with Tom as he ran over to gather it in.

Kit went on counting his motions, thinking only of throwing the ball hard and straight and over the plate. It worked. He got it right over the middle of the plate every time. The trouble was that three batters in a row swung their bats over the middle of the plate at the instant his pitch arrived. Three almost identical drives carried nearly to the fence, and three runs scored.

Then time was called, and Mr. Ginger walked toward the mound. Kit held the ball out to him. "I told you I was no pitcher," he said. "I haven't got a ball past the batter yet. And it looks like I wouldn't if I stood here all day. Who's relieving?"

Mr. Ginger shook his head. "Nobody. You'll be all right if you calm down and use your head. Don't you know what you're doing, Kit? You're putting every pitch in exactly the same place at exactly the same speed. Any halfway good batter can hit it.

And when he hits a straight, fast ball like that, it really goes. I don't expect you to know how to throw curves or cut corners. But you can let go a little sooner or a little later, and you can pitch a little harder or a little easier. Just vary your timing enough so the batters can't figure it so perfectly. Then even if a batter does hit the ball, somebody may be able to field it. Come on, Kit. We all know you can do it."

Kit nodded solemnly. Next time he eased up just a bit as he threw. The batter connected. But, as Mr. Ginger had predicted, the ball didn't take off. The batter had topped it instead of hitting it square-ly, and it came along the ground right at Kit. He scooped it up and flipped it to Tom.

He did the same thing next time. It worked again, but this time the ball bounced toward the shortstop. Kit leaped to his right to grab it and threw to Tom again. The inning was over.

Kit singled in the bottom of the inning, scoring Tony who had reached first on an error and ad-vanced on two walks. Then, in the third, Kit doubled to drive in Bruce and Tom, both of whom had walked. That tied the score.

Meanwhile, Kit tried to use his head on the mound. Varying his timing and discovering how he could control the path of the ball by the slightest difference in the way he moved his body, he found himself miraculously able to keep the Bears from scoring again. They hit his pitches but never exactly right. They got on base, but someone always managed to get the third out before anyone crossed the plate.

The score was still tied at the end of the fifth. "Thought you told me you weren't a pitcher!" Mr. Ginger slapped Kit on the back as he flopped down on the bench. Kit winced. He was tired enough to drop. His arm ached, and he had an awful pain in his stomach. But he managed to grin.

"If we can pick up a run in this inning and hold them in their half, you'll be a *winning* pitcher," Mr. Ginger exulted. "Of course, if we go into extra innings, you'll have to come out."

Kit had forgotten the rule about not pitching more than six innings. Suddenly he felt very much like a pitcher, and more than anything he wanted to be a winning one. But the chances didn't look bright. The weak end of the batting order was coming up— chubby Mike Parsons; Lew Kingsley, with an unbroken string of strikeouts; and Ralph DeForest, who had once managed to beat out a single. If only the inning would last long enough to let him get to bat, Kit resolved that he would get a hit or die trying. But he was sixth in line.

"Make him pitch to you, Mike! Don't swing unless it's in there," Kit yelled ferociously. Mike had a horrible habit of swinging at any pitch, bad or good. This time he held off and got a walk.

In spite of the same cautioning words Lew struck out, and so did Ralph. Although Sam Holland carried himself like a hitter, so far he hadn't had much luck.

"Come on, Sam! You can do it," Kit cried. Sam grinned, took two called strikes, and then belted one past second for a clean single. A good runner would have gone from first to third on it, but Mike was lucky to make second.

Now it was up to Tom. Kit got to his feet, jammed on a helmet, and grabbed a couple of bats. "Now's your chance, Tom. Be a hero!" he called. With men on base Tom was in his glory. And he really was a pretty good hitter.

Tom crouched at the plate, waggling his bat jauntily. He took a ball, low. Then he swung and sent up a soft fly that dropped in front of the right fielder.

Kit ground his teeth in frustration. With anybody but Mike on base, those two hits would have brought in a run. Mike looked overjoyed to be at third. Still this was Kit's chance to be a hero, with the bases loaded and two out.

Kit took a called strike and then a ball high. He swung at the next pitch and sent it hard down the third-base line. He rounded first, smiling happily as he watched Mike cross the plate. Then the umpire called "Foul ball!" With a groan, Kit trotted back and picked up the bat again.

The next pitch looked pretty good, but he let it go by. It was a ball, just inside. The next pitch was fat and perfect. He swung, felt the clean tingle up his arms, and ran. When he had a chance to look, the ball was bouncing across the grass on the other side of the fence. He had hit a home run! A yell of triumph went up from the bleachers. Kit was racing for the plate when he saw the umpire waving him back, holding up two fingers. After a furious moment, he realized what that meant. The ball had bounced over, and that made his hit a double. But two runs had scored, and that should be enough.

When Bruce struck out to end the inning, Kit trotted in happily. Now all he needed to do was to hold the Bears to one run.

For the first time he felt at ease on the mound. Instead of keeping his eyes fixed on the plate, he let them wander to the bleachers. He spotted some friends and his parents. His father was beaming proudly, and his mother's cheeks were pink with excitement. Suddenly Kit had a feeling as if the earth had dropped from under him. The ball fell from his hand, and he had to fumble for it on the ground. Then he straightened up and looked again, hoping his eyes had deceived him.

They hadn't. Miss Rogers and her tiny withered-looking friend were sitting on the front row of the bleachers. Miss Rogers was leaning forward with her hands clasped on top of her cane, staring at him with a grim, witch-like expression. The smaller lady was sitting with folded arms and thin lips clamped tightly together.

He'd forgotten! He'd been yelling at the batters, full volume. The crowd had forgotten and exploded in cheers when it seemed that he had hit a grand slammer. Now the old ladies had come, slipping up when he wasn't looking. No doubt they were angry with Mr. Benjamin for giving the Little Leaguers a second chance and were going to make sure it didn't happen again.

Kit's happiness drained away, as well as his self-confidence. Once more he felt shaky, but now he was too tired to brace himself against it. His first pitch was weak enough for a baby to hit, but luckily the batter reached for it and lofted it into the air. Ralph had time to get under it.

The next hitter had more patience and a sharper eye. He waited for a good pitch, and Kit didn't have one in him. The batter walked, and so did the next one.

Kit looked pleadingly at Mr. Ginger, but Mr. Ginger just smiled. There was no escape. In desperation Kit concentrated on getting the ball over the plate no matter how. The next batter hit a double to drive in the tying runs. The next hit was a long drive that landed just inside the fence and bounced over.

82

That was it. The Bears joyfully threw their caps into the air. The Colts plodded off the field with heads bowed.

Kit's father threw an arm around his shoulders and said, "Good try, Kit. You came awfully close." When Kit didn't reply he gave him a little squeeze and said, "We'll pick up some peppermint ice cream on the way home. See you later."

Kit tried to smile. He knew his parents were being kind. Even though peppermint ice cream was his favorite food, it couldn't make him happy now. Why, he had just thrown away a game that the Colts had as good as won. More than that, he'd thrown away the rest of the season for everybody, just because he had forgotten to keep his big mouth shut.

When Kit had a chance to look around, the old ladies were making their feeble way back toward the house. Nobody looked particularly downhearted, even the Colts.

"Good going, Kit," Tom told him. The rest of the boys joined in with assurances that he had done a good job.

"We came awfully close," Mr. Ginger said. "You played a good game, fellows, especially considering the way we had to juggle our lineup at the last minute. Web, you did a fine job. And Kit, I'm proud of you. For a first start, you came through in great shape. Now, don't forget the game on Sunday. We won't have a chance to practice before then, so everybody be here early for a good warm-up."

Kit thought about the old ladies. They hadn't said anything after all! Then why had they come? Scowling in the direction of the house where the two figures were just disappearing through the door, Kit made up his mind exactly why. First Mr. Benjamin had jinxed him, but this time he had sent Miss Rogers and her friend.

He had been right in the beginning. This was going to be his unlucky season. It wasn't bad enough to be stuck with number thirteen on his uniform. He had to have these grouchy-looking old people showing up every time it was important for him to play his best. Of course they had a right to come if they wanted to. After all, it *was* their field. For some reason, making himself be fair to them had the effect of lifting his spirits. He enjoyed his peppermint ice cream after all, although he was so tired that his mother accused him of trying to sleep at the dinner table.

Chapter 12

A Final Proof

NEXT MORNING, the first thing Kit heard was his mother's voice telling him that if he didn't get up right away he would be late for school. Her exasperated tone warned him that she had tried several times to get him up.

Kit groaned, and started to sit up. Then he groaned louder and fell back again. Every muscle in his body ached, especially the muscles across his stomach. He was more exhausted than he had ever been in his life, except for the time a couple of years before when he had had a bad case of flu.

He burrowed his face lazily into the pillow. If he had been coming down with some sickness yesterday, nobody could blame him for losing the game. He wouldn't have to worry about being jinxed, either. People got sick all the time, and it was nobody's fault.

But he knew that if he missed school on Friday,

his mother would make him stay in the house over the weekend no matter how much better he felt. Gritting his teeth, he forced himself out of bed and into his clothes. The Colts had a game Sunday, and he couldn't miss that.

When Kit was up he felt better. By the time he had finished breakfast, he knew that there was nothing wrong with him except some very sore muscles.

"I hope I never have to pitch again," he groaned to Bill at recess. "I expected my arm to be sore, but I never thought I'd feel like this."

"Don't worry," Bill said. "Next time it won't be so bad. It's because you were so nervous you tensed up all over. You'll get used to it."

"Not me!" Kit shook his head emphatically. "Pitching! You can have it."

"You'd feel different if we'd won yesterday."

Kit shook his head, but he knew that Bill was right. He remembered his good feeling when the game seemed won and his soaring pride at the thought of winning his first start. "That's the only good thing about losing," he said. "Mr. Ginger will never ask me to pitch again."

"You weren't so bad," Bill said judiciously. "Once you got over that first inning, you did fine. Only you got tired right at the end. Those things happen."

"Yeah, tired," Kit agreed. But he knew he hadn't felt tired, at least not until the game ended and the let-down came. What had finished him had been the sight of those old ladies. If they had stayed home, he could have won.

By Sunday Kit felt almost as good as new. He could ignore the lingering soreness in his muscles, especially since he was back behind the plate. Bill was pitching, starting a new week.

Bill's pitching made all the difference. A couple of Lions got on base in the first but failed to score. In the bottom of the inning, the Colts went down in order. In the top of the second, the third out came with bases loaded, but again no Lion had crossed the plate.

Leading off the second, Kit stood well back in the box. The Lions' pitcher had struck out Bill, Tony, and Tom on speed alone. Kit wanted as much time as possible to get around on those fast pitches. He watched two strikes go by. The next time he swung late and sent the ball into the bleachers behind first base. The next he dropped into right field for a single.

Bruce struck out, but a fumble by the Lions' catcher let Kit go to second. Then Sam Holland singled with a grounder over second, and Kit went to third. Ralph sent a lazy hopper toward the mound. Kit was off so fast that the only play was to first. That made two outs, but Kit had brought in a run.

The Lions' pitcher, who at first had seemed unhittable, had by this time lost a bit of his speed and more than a bit of his self-confidence. The Colts, encouraged by Kit's and Sam's examples, found their batting eyes sharpened by their rising spirits. Ted Erhart sent a hard liner down the third base line that brought in Sam with the second run. Martin Woolsey walked. When the Lions' shortstop fumbled Bill's grounder, the bases were loaded. Tony sent a long fly soaring toward the fence, and the Colts rejoiced at the prospect of a really big inning. But a leaping grab by the Lions' center fielder ended it abruptly.

Through all the excitement, the players and spectators had managed to moderate their cries of joy or dismay. They had kept their applause gentle and polite. There had been no noise loud enough to reach the ears of the people at the Marley Home, and everyone seemed determined that there wouldn't be.

From behind the plate, Kit had the big house right before his eyes. Without missing any of the action on the field, he could keep it under constant observation. Nobody could slip up on him as the two old ladies had done while he was pitching. This time he would be able to see anyone coming and would have time to brace himself against any bad luck that might be on the way.

Bill started the third inning by giving up a hit

to the Lions' right fielder. That was no great surprise, for he was the only left-handed batter in the lineup and Bill had always found pitching to left-handers difficult. Bill gave special attention next to the Lions' cleanup hitter and struck him out with one of his rarely-used curves. But when he tried the same thing on the next batter, something happened. Instead of breaking away from the batter and over the plate, the ball veered farther to the inside and thumped smartly against the batter's leg.

Time was called while the Lions' manager ran to examine the injured leg. Kit took advantage of the pause to trot to the mound.

Bill looked pale and shaky. "Is he hurt, Kit?" he asked anxiously. Even more than most pitchers, Bill dreaded hitting a batter.

Kit shook his head. "He's all right." The batter was on his feet, rubbing his leg. "He'll be running like a rabbit if he gets a chance. Just don't let it bother you. Keep putting the ball in the strike zone and let the batters worry about staying out of the way."

But as Kit had feared, Bill couldn't shake off his nervousness. Shying away from the inside half of the plate, he walked the next batter on four outside pitches. That loaded the bases.

By asking the umpire to examine the ball, pretending to adjust the buckles of his shin guards, and giving non-existent signals so Bill would have to shake them off and wait for new ones, Kit did all he could to waste time and give Bill a chance to settle down. It worked well enough to gain a second strikeout. But then the Lions' pitcher hit a weak grounder that died halfway between third base and the mound. Bill, who should have fielded it, stood staring as he tried to make up his mind what to do. With a runner on his way from third, Kit dared not leave the plate. By the time Sam and Ralph decided to try for it, there was no play anywhere. The Lions scored a run, and the bases were still loaded.

"Don't let it bother you, Bill," Kit called cheerfully. "Nobody could be that lucky twice. Put it right past him. He can't hit what he can't see."

Bill blinked and set his jaw determinedly. He threw something he practiced a lot but seldom used, a real let-up pitch. The batter swung too soon, reached awkwardly, and with the tip of his bat nudged the ball toward first. Tom scooped it up without stepping off the bag. That ended the Lions' threat, at least for the time being.

As things turned out, it was ended for good. Kit basked in the satisfaction that comes when everything is going exactly as it should. Bill was pitching as he usually did when things were going smoothly. With Bill able to put the ball exactly where he wanted it every time, catching was a breeze. Bill might be a poor hitter and an absolutely impossible fielder, but he was the best Little League hurler around. Kit would have asked nothing better than to have him pitch every game.

Kit's happiness was complete when he led off the fifth with a double and then scored the Colts' third run on Ralph's single. That gave him two hits for three times at bat.

Then Bill disposed of the Lions with a grounder to first, a strikeout, and a grounder to second. It was a satisfying sort of game that was close enough to be exciting but not close enough to be really nerve-racking.

Everyone had played well, but Kit took quiet satisfaction in the fact that he had kept the team on its winning course. Bill was getting the back-slapping and the compliments and would be credited for the win, but Kit didn't mind. He knew that he had done a good job. Also, he had the casual, quiet commendation of the people who counted—Mr. Ginger and the other team's manager, his fellow players, and especially his own father. Taken all together, this had been a perfect day.

Kit was convinced that he knew exactly why it had been perfect. Not one of those old people had set foot out of their house. Not one had come to glare at him disapprovingly and remind him of how soft and lazy and spoiled he was supposed to be. If he had needed proof that the people who lived in the Marley Home were responsible for his bad luck, he had it now.

Chapter 13

Mr. Benjamin Sounds Off

Tuesday Bob was back in school, looking a little pale. Kit breathed a sigh of relief. Bill wasn't eligible to pitch in tomorrow's game, so it was really important for Bob to be there. He had beaten the Stags in the first game and should be able to do it again.

"I won't be at the game," Tony announced as he, Kit, and Tom headed home after school. "Dad's clerk, Mr. Martin, is sick; and there's no time to find anybody else."

"Too bad!" Tom said sympathetically.

"Hope you can make the next game," Kit added.

But when Tony left, they agreed that the Colts wouldn't miss him much. "He's about as graceful as an ox," Tom laughed, "and just as fast. I'm surprised every time he makes a catch."

"But he *does* make most of 'em," Kit protested.

"Anyway, the important thing is that Bob is back. Don't know what we'd do if he wasn't around to pitch."

When they got to the field on Wednesday, the first thing Mr. Ginger did was to beckon Kit to one side. "You'll pitch today," he said.

"Me?" Kit wailed. "I told you, Mr. Ginger. I'm no pitcher. Look how I messed up the last game. I thought it would be Bob."

Mr. Ginger shook his head. "Bob still looks a little peaked. I don't think he's up to it. As for you, Kit, you're a better pitcher than you think. You had a bad case of stage fright last time, but you lived through six innings. This time will be easier."

As Kit started warming up, the things he had learned in the panic and misery of his first start began to come back. Everything really was easier. Soon he stopped thinking about the bad part of the game he had pitched and remembered those innings when he had felt himself firmly in command. He made up his mind that this time it would be that way all through.

Then he remembered that once more he would have his back to the big house. Someone might sneak up on him again while he wasn't looking. But they had all stayed away last time. Maybe there was no reason to worry about them any more.

93

The Colts were first up, Tom leading off. He started the game with a clean single up the middle. Bruce, who had moved to center to replace Tony, walked. Sam struck out, and then it was Kit's chance to give himself a starting edge. He took a called strike, followed by a ball, inside. The next pitch he swung on and drove past the shortstop for a single that scored Tom with the first run.

Bob walked. Then Ted slammed a double against the fence. Kit tore around third with a broad grin on his face and followed Bruce across the plate. That made three, probably all for this time. Lew and Ralph were up next, and neither was much of a hitter. But Lew was lucky. The Stags' second baseman fumbled his grounder, and the bases were loaded.

Kit whooped with joy, but softly. He had visions of a really big lead, a lead so overwhelming that he could relax and enjoy sharpening up his pitching. "Way to go, Ralphie," he called as Ralph drove the first pitch straight at the second baseman.

Usually when a player made an error, he would become so rattled that he would fumble worse than ever on the next play. But this time it didn't work that way. The boy grabbed the ball, stepped on the base, and threw to first in one fiercely determined movement. That ended the Colts' big inning. But a three-run lead ought to be enough for anybody.

Once he took the mound, Kit became completely absorbed in trying to remember how to pitch to each batter. By concentrating on how to make the ball do what he wanted, he had no time to think about the Marley Home people or anything else. He even began to understand why good pitchers sometimes weren't very good hitters. When his team was at bat, he couldn't stop thinking of the hitters he would pitch to in the next inning.

Though it wasn't the misery it had been in his first start, pitching still wasn't easy. Kit made the mistake of underrating the wispy little second baseman who led off by giving him a fat pitch that he dropped behind third for a single. He put everything he had into striking out the Stags' first baseman, a big, hard-hitting left-hander. He took the third baseman to a three-and-two count. Then, in an all-out effort to avoid walking him, he put a pitch so carefully across the middle that the batter sent it soaring over his head to drop just out of Bruce's reach. The fleet little second baseman went to third, though Bruce's quick recovery held the batter at first.

Kit looked at the runner on first, then at the one on third.

"One out, you guys!" Web called.

Everybody knew what to expect. The infielders moved in, poised on the balls of their feet and ready to move fast.

Keep the pitches up, Kit thought. But the first two were a little too far up. When he tried to make the next one a bit lower, the batter caught it against a bat held just right. It trickled with maddening slowness toward the mound. Kit darted for it, bent, and grabbed; but he knew it was too late for a play at home. He threw to Tom for the second out, but his nice three-run lead had already been cut to two.

He kept it at that when he grabbed a hard bouncer off the bat of the next hitter for the third out.

Hits by Bruce, Ted, and Ralph gave the Colts two more runs in the top of the second to increase Kit's lead to four. The Stags came back with two and erased the advantage.

It was in the bottom of the third with the Colts still leading five to three when Kit found himself once again possessed by that glorious feeling of being in command. All at once the baseball wasn't an object he had to control. It was part of him, like his hand. He didn't need to think about it any more than he thought about his feet when he ran. He could give his whole mind to the battle with the hitter.

Through the third and the fourth everything was smooth sailing. Batters clubbed the ball to the ground or popped it into the air. Nobody got good wood on it. Kit felt that he could go all day without giving the Stags a chance to catch up.

Then, as he strolled in to lead off the fifth, he

stopped short and stared in astonishment at the bleachers. They had sneaked up on him again. This time it wasn't just Mr. Benjamin or a couple of old ladies. Sitting on the front row of the bleachers were—he counted quickly—ten old people.

Mr. Benjamin was back, and on one side of him was that gaunt scarecrow, Mr. McIntyre. On his other side was Miss Rogers with her tiny friend. The others were people he had met that awful evening, but he had already forgotten their names. All their faces were set in expressions of grim disapproval.

What could have happened to bring so many of them here? He could think of nothing anybody had done to bring such an invasion.

This was the end. Twice before the team had escaped. But this was the third strike, and after it the Millbrook Little League would be out for good.

Kit let the dreadful prospect distract him so much that for the first time all season he went down on strikes without lifting the bat from his shoulder. Bob also struck out, and Ted lifted an easy fly over center field. Before Kit had a chance to collect his thoughts, he was on the mound again.

All the skill that Kit had learned so painfully deserted him. His mind was a blank. When he managed to throw the ball, the result didn't even deserve to be called a pitch. It was just a weak, characterless toss that any beginner might have been ashamed of. The batter drove it past Bob for a single. The next batter repeated the performance, and there were two on.

Kit wanted to throw down his glove and walk away. But nobody did that, no matter how bad things were. He looked pleadingly at Mr. Ginger, but Mr. Ginger was making no move to get ready another pitcher.

Even Web didn't seem to realize how hopelessly Kit had collapsed. He called cheerfully, "Lucky hits, that's all. Don't let it bother you!"

The next batter watched Kit's feeble pitch fade and drop, bounce on the plate and out of Web's reach. The runners went to second and third while he chased it down.

"PUT SOME STEAM BEHIND THOSE PITCHES, BOY!" The ear-shattering roar almost lifted Kit off the mound. He looked around wildly, wondering who could be so ignorant or so heedless.

Everybody was staring in amazement at the person who had dared to shatter the firmly established quiet. It was easy to see who had done it but hard to believe. On his feet, red-faced and shaking a clenched fist in the direction of the mound, was Mr. Benjamin.

Beside him Miss Rogers leaned forward, seeming in danger of toppling off the bench. "My goodness, Christopher!" she shrilled fiercely. "You've got this game won. Don't throw it away now."

Such relief surged through Kit that he could hardly keep from laughing out loud. They hadn't come to complain at all. They had come to watch the game! And, though he could hardly believe it, they wanted him to win.

Even more rapidly than it had ebbed, strength flowed back into Kit. Once more the ball was like part of him. With an ease that surprised him, he struck out the next three batters.

He didn't worry when his teammates couldn't score in the top of the sixth. Again he set the Stags down in order, and the game was won.

As Kit came in from the mound, Mr. Benjamin grabbed his hand and shook it vigorously. "Great game, son. Just great!" he cried. "Hope I didn't make you nervous, yelling out like that. Baseball crowds have sure changed since my day. We tried to keep quiet like the rest of the folks, but I just got carried away. Miss Rogers, too."

"No, *sir!*" Kit shook his head emphatically. "It was just what I needed. Sort of woke me up, you might say. Thanks a lot."

Kit's father and a couple of other Little League officials came rushing over. Looking embarrassed and yet amused, they explained, "It's not that baseball crowds have changed that much, sir. We must have misunderstood you when you told us you didn't want a lot of noise and disturbance if you let the boys use the field. We gave everybody strict orders not to yell or cheer so we wouldn't disturb you."

Mr. Benjamin and the others laughed. "That wasn't what we meant at all," Mr. Benjamin said.

"I should say not!" Miss Rogers exclaimed. "All we meant was that we didn't want the young people crowding in here all hours of the day or night raising a ruckus. We've been out of touch with children so long, we hardly knew what to expect. But, my goodness! A ball game's not a ball game if people can't let loose and yell when they feel like it."

Chapter 14

A Happy Surprise

"SIT RIGHT HERE, LEW." Mrs. Dawson indicated a chair just inside Kit's door. "I don't want you catching Kit's germs."

"I'll be careful, Mrs. Dawson," Lew said meekly. Kit knew he must have come straight from the field, for he still was wearing his uniform and his face was flushed and streaked with dust.

"What happened?" demanded Kit. Missing one of the Colts' games was something he hadn't thought he would ever do, but he had been knocked flat by a virus. Yesterday he had felt so miserable he hadn't even been able to worry about missing the fun of the last day of school. Today he had recovered enough to fret about being unable to play. He had been hoping that somebody would remember to stop and tell him about the game. But why was it Lew Kingsley instead of Tom or Tony?

"It was a funny game with our best players missing," Lew began.

"Best players? Who?"

"Well—you, of course. And Tom, and Tony, and Bill. All the big kids we count on most," Lew explained.

"What happened to everybody?"

"Bill turned his ankle stepping off the stage at the end-of-school program yesterday. You know he's always having accidents. Tony had to help his father in the store. And I guess you know about Tom."

"What about Tom?" Kit wondered what awful thing could have happened to Tom while he had been sick and cut off from the world.

"You remember. Back when we didn't have a field and nobody thought we'd play this year, Tom's parents arranged for him to go to summer camp. Tom figured it was all off, but a couple of days ago his parents told him he had to go. They had already paid some money they couldn't get back, and they had made plans for things they wanted to do while he was gone. I guess he's halfway there by now."

"Tough luck!" Kit shook his head sympathetically. He felt very sorry for Tom, but he remembered how Tom had pleaded to go to camp though he knew his parents really couldn't afford to send him. Maybe it served Tom right to have to go. However, his departure left the Colts short a first baseman.

"Who played first?" Kit asked.

"Ralph." The way Lew said it made Kit feel sure

that Ralph's performance had left much to be desired.

"He wasn't so hot?"

Lew shook his head. "But then nobody else was, either."

"I suppose Bob pitched," Kit guessed.

Lew shook his head. "No, I did. Mr. Ginger didn't think Bob was well enough yet. But sick or not, he couldn't have done worse than I did."

"Sounds like we lost." Kit really expected it since the Tigers had beaten the Colts before.

"We sure did. It was a real mess. Twelve to two. They hit everything I threw. But on top of that, you never saw so many errors. Ralph made a couple. Sam was at third, and he muffed just about every chance he got. They were playing positions they weren't used to, so they had some excuse. But Ted's played second all along, and he made a couple, too. Bruce did all right in center, but he twisted his ankle in the fourth inning. Mr. Ginger put Mike in. Right off, he dropped an easy fly and let in two runs. It got so bad it was almost funny."

"If we had to lose, maybe it was a good thing to get all those errors out of our systems in one game," Kit said lightly.

Lew groaned. "Easy for you to talk. You didn't have to suffer through it. The worst thing was having such a big crowd watching. All those old people were there."

"More than last time?"

"A dozen at least," Lew said. "You know that tall old lady, Miss Rogers? She asked where you were. Said to tell you to hurry up and get well." Kit couldn't help feeling pleased that Miss Rogers had missed him.

The first thing Kit did when he arrived at the field Friday for the game against the Wildcats was to look around for Miss Rogers. But the bleachers were empty. Although it was too early for spectators, Mr. Benjamin was talking with Mr. Ginger and the Wildcats' manager, Mr. Roe. Kit hadn't recognized Mr. Benjamin at first because he was wearing a funny-looking old baseball cap. It was faded blue with "M.C." on it in white letters.

"Howdy, son," Mr. Benjamin called. "So you're able to navigate again, eh? Maybe we'll have a ball game today instead of a massacre."

"I guess the Colts had bad luck last time," Kit said. "We'll try to make this game interesting for you."

Mr. Benjamin shook his head sternly. "Don't worry about whether it's interesting. Keep your mind on business and think about beating that other team. Never mind who's watching."

"Yes, sir," Kit said.

"Bob seems to be in shape again," Mr. Ginger

said. "Better start getting him warmed up, Kit."

It felt good to buckle on the chest protector and shin guards, ready to get behind the plate. As Bob warmed up, his pitches smacked into the mitt just as they had before he came down with the measles.

Tony and Bruce were in their old places in the outfield with Ralph at third. In fact, all the Colts' lineup was back to normal except that Tom was missing from first. They would have to get used to that, for he would be at camp until the season ended. In his place was Bill, whose height and long reach should help him do a good job. But who would take over when Bill pitched? Kit decided not to worry about it. That was Mr. Ginger's job.

The Colts had finished their warm-up, and the Wildcats were starting theirs when Kit saw the Marley Home people coming. There was quite a crowd of them. They moved more briskly than before and had an altogether different look.

Some of the men were carrying folding chairs. A couple had thermos jugs, and one had a wicker basket. A plump, white-haired lady held a pink parasol, and the light shining through it almost made her face look young. They settled down, some in the bleachers and some in the folding chairs. They smiled and spoke to the people around them instead of sitting in grim silence as before.

Kit looked for Miss Rogers. When he spotted her, he waved and smiled. She waved back. In spite of Mr. Benjamin's advice, Kit resolved that he would show her that the Colts might be beaten but not trampled over like last time.

When the game started, it looked as if the Colts would have trouble proving anything to anybody. The Wildcats had come up with a left-handed pitcher who struck out Ralph, Tony, and Bruce without even seeming to try.

Bob's pitches, on the other hand, seemed made to order for the Wildcats. The lead-off batter sent a drive down the third base line that only a sensational leap by Ralph kept from going for a double. Bob pitched too cautiously to the next batter and ended by walking him. The number three man slammed a hard grounder down the middle, putting himself on first and the front runner on third.

The Wildcats' cleanup hitter was their catcher, a hulking, muscular boy who could put the ball out of sight. Kit groaned. Then he had a sudden hunch. He called time and trotted to the mound.

"In a spot like this Mr. Roe generally calls for a bunt," Kit said. "Let's make it easy. The infield's sharp today. They'll get you out of it."

"Okay, Kit." Bob's face brightened.

Kit wasn't as confident as he sounded. Suppose he had guessed wrong and that big kid slammed Bob's easy pitch out of the park? Bob would never trust him again.

But, as in the first game, Kit was lucky. The big

slugger did try a bunt, and Bob had made it so easy he couldn't miss. As Kit had hoped, this kid wasn't good at bunting. He probably had hoped to get a couple of strikes on him so that he would have an excuse to hit away. His awkward, half-hearted attempt popped the ball high enough into the air so that Sam, running hard, could get his glove under it. The runner on third who had started for home dived hastily back.

Flushed with triumph, Bob set down the next two batters. The inning was over, and the Wildcats hadn't scored.

Kit led off the second, determined to show the other Colts that the Wildcats' left-hander wasn't so tough. He took a called strike, a ball, a second called strike, and a second ball. He swung and popped a foul over the backstop and then sent another soaring into the pine trees behind the bleachers. Each time he got a little more feeling of being able to judge the pitches as they came in. He swung again, ran, and found himself safe at first.

What seemed like a solid wave of noise swept over him. For a moment Kit was scared, and his eyes flew apprehensively toward the big house. Then he remembered that most of the people who lived there were at the field. He turned toward the place where he had seen them settle down before the game. But they didn't look settled now, and they didn't look annoyed by the deafening roar that filled this

107

usually quiet place. They couldn't look annoyed, because they were the ones who were making most of the noise. They were on their feet, yelling at the tops of their voices. Miss Rogers was adding to the racket by pounding on a bench with her cane, and the old lady with the parasol was waving it in wild circles above her head.

Kit's face grew hot, and he knew that it was turning bright red. From all the fuss, anybody would have thought he had hit a grand-slam home run instead of just a plain single.

But though it was only a single, Kit's hit had broken the left-hander's spell. Bob didn't let himself be tempted by bad pitches as the batters had in the first inning. He drew a walk. When Ted smashed a double against the center field fence, Kit sped across the plate with the Colts' first run.

After that the game settled down to a nip-and-tuck affair that the Colts won by a score of seven to six. It was a good feeling to win. But even better was the feeling of freedom. Today's game had been just like the ones at the old field. Everyone had been able to let go and act natural.

"Boys! Boys!" The players had been discussing the game excitedly while helping to gather up the equipment and were startled at the sound of Miss Rogers' voice. Were they to be scolded now for the commotion they had caused?

But Miss Rogers was smiling. She said in a

strangely shy voice, "We thought you might like some refreshment after playing so hard." Set out on the bench were the thermos jugs, stacks of paper cups, and several plates heaped with cookies.

"There's lemonade in this jug and fruit punch in the other," said the tiniest of the old ladies.

"Try the cookies," coaxed the lady with the parasol. "We baked them this morning, so they're nice and fresh."

As Kit sipped his lemonade, which was ice-cold and exactly as sweet as he liked it, he gazed thoughtfully at the Marley Home people. They really seemed like friends now, and he wondered how he could ever have been afraid of them. Suddenly a surprising idea popped into his head. Maybe he really was the one who had gotten the field for the Millbrook Little League. Maybe the people at the Marley Home had never heard about the kids needing a field until he told them. Maybe they talked it over after he was gone and decided to help. The more he thought about it, the more convinced Kit became that that was exactly what had happened. He wished that, without seeming boastful, he could let people know what he had done.

Chapter 15

Mr. Benjamin Chases a Jinx

"You're not mad, are you?" Tony asked anxiously.

Kit shook his head. "Of course not. There's no law says you've got to play baseball."

"My father didn't make me quit," Tony went on. "Didn't even ask me to. But we found out that Mr. Martin's going to be laid up most of the summer. And now, when we're getting ready to move to the new shopping center, Dad doesn't have time to break in new help. So I figured it was up to me."

"Sure, I understand," Kit said. Most of Kit's friends had switched ambitions from day to day—from cowboy to fireman, from big-league ball player to astronaut, from movie star to explorer. But Tony had never wanted to do anything but run Sheldon's Hardware Store, as his father did now and his grandfather also had done.

Tony started learning hardware even before he started to school. He could locate any item in the store down to the smallest nail and the newest variety of insect spray. Kit knew that Tony was really happy to play an important part in the family business.

"We'll miss you," Kit said, "but the store's really important to your family. Right now it looks as if your family needs you even more than the team does."

After the conversation with Tony, Kit wandered over to the ball park although he was more than an hour early for the warm-up. Mr. Benjamin was there raking up twigs and bits of paper from the field. Kit went over to help him.

While they worked together, Kit found himself describing in detail his talk with Tony. Kit was surprised at how easy it was to talk to Mr. Benjamin.

Mr. Benjamin said, "Sonny, if you don't make it as a ball player, you ought to be a diplomat. You've made your friend feel that he's important to the team and will be missed. Still he doesn't have to worry that the boys will be mad at him or feel guilty about doing what he wants."

They worked on a few moments, and then Mr. Benjamin said, "But suppose you were in Tony's place? For you, it wouldn't be so easy to quit baseball, would it?"

"I think I'd do what Tony did if Dad really needed me. But I'm glad I don't have to," Kit admitted. "I'd just about die if I had to quit the team."

"And your team would just about die, too." Mr. Benjamin straightened up and surveyed the field critically. "Guess that's taken care of." He groaned slightly as he settled onto the bench. Kit dropped down beside him.

"Yes, sir!" Mr. Benjamin went on. "Your Colts will manage fine without your friend. Oh, he's a nice enough boy, but no ball player. He's too slow. And that smart-alecky first baseman—he's gone for good, too?"

"Honest, Mr. Benjamin," Kit protested, "Tom's not really a smart aleck. He's a good kid when you get to know him."

"I just go by what I see on the field. That boy's a showoff. He's not a bad player, but he's too flashy. He makes an easy play look hard to get people to notice him. You'll be surprised how well you get along without him. But if it were you, Kit—but that's another story! You're holding that team together. If you'd seen them that day you were home sick, you'd know what I mean."

Kit fidgeted uneasily, pleased yet embarrassed by Mr. Benjamin's praise. At last he mumbled, "I'm surprised when I do anything right with this jinx number I've got. I'll probably break a leg before the season's over."

Mr. Benjamin looked surprised. "Does wearing thirteen really bother you?"

"Not all the time. Mostly I forget about it. But when something bad happens, I think about it and get scared. Like—you know—maybe this is it."

Mr. Benjamin shook his head wonderingly. "The way you've been playing, I'd have sworn you knew," he said.

"Knew what?"

"Why, that thirteen's the luckiest number you can have. *If* you know how to make it work for you, that is. Now, when I was with the Millbrook Cougars, back in 1910 . . . "

"The Millbrook Cougars?" Kit had been taught not to interrupt people, but he wanted to know what Mr. Benjamin was talking about.

"You never heard of the Millbrook Cougars? Well, that was long before your time. Those days we didn't have television or radio or fast cars to rush to the city when we wanted some fun. We had to make our excitement right here. So every town had its baseball team. Towns as large as Millbrook had regular professional teams. I was catcher for the Cougars for eight seasons, starting in 1909."

Kit stared at Mr. Benjamin in awestruck silence. So that was why the old man had been able to put that first ball so briskly over the plate. No wonder he could judge players so casually and so keenly. And that funny-looking old cap must be the one that he had worn years ago. Kit had been interested in what Mr. Benjamin had to say before, but now he listened with rapt attention.

"There was a fellow started out with me," Mr. Benjamin went on. "Mike O'Meara was his name. Real superstitious fellow. He had a certain bat that was the only one he'd use. If he spilled the salt at breakfast or had a black cat run in front of him, his whole day was ruined. He wasn't a bad player, but somehow he couldn't find a spot for himself. His first season he mostly rode the bench. Second season, he was barely hanging on. He got to be kind of the goat for the whole team. The fellows were always playing jokes on him, and I was as bad as the next man.

"One day we came up with what we thought was a whale of an idea. We got hold of Mike's uniform, and our third baseman talked his girl into ripping off the number and sewing on a big thirteen. We figured that'd scare the daylights out of him. Well, what do you reckon happened?"

Kit shook his head. "What?"

"The very next day our third baseman started out to his girl's house to take her for a buggy ride. The horse bolted, and the poor fellow wound up with a broken leg. Our manager put in O'Meara just to fill in while he looked around for a third baseman. But O'Meara did such a bang-up job that after a few games he had the position nailed down. Before the

114

season was over a scout from the Big State League spotted him and signed him up. A couple of seasons later he was playing for Chicago in the World Series."

"All because of that thirteen?"

Mr. Benjamin chuckled. "Who knows? The thing is, Mike O'Meara was even more superstitious than we thought. What we didn't know was that Mike thought that while thirteen might be unlucky for everybody else, it was lucky for him. His idea was that just one thirteen is a jinx, all right. But if you put a lot of thirteens together you make it *your* number. Then it's lucky for you. Now Mike's birthday was the thirteenth of May, and he had thirteen letters in his name."

Kit frowned and counted on his fingers to be sure. "Mike O'Meara? That's only ten."

"Ah, but his real name was Michael. That's thirteen. So when he found that thirteen on his suit, instead of being scared he was tickled to death. Now a sensible person like you or me would know that number didn't have a thing to do with that third baseman breaking his leg and giving Mike a chance at his job. But Mike just knew that it did. He got to be a regular fanatic about thirteens. He'd make sure to have thirteen coins in his pocket. He'd have thirteen buttons on his clothes, even if he had to sew a couple of extras on his underwear. He'd figure where to stand so he could take thirteen steps to the plate. Yes, sir! Mike O'Meara was a real character."

Kit had been so absorbed in Mr. Benjamin's story that he hadn't noticed the other players arriving. When it ended, he had to hurry away and start to warm up. But the story stayed in his mind.

Could thirteen be lucky for him as it had been for Mike O'Meara? His birthday wasn't the thirteenth, and there was no way he could juggle his name to make the letters add up to thirteen. But he was going on thirteen years old, and this was the thirteenth season for the Millbrook Little League. Before the game started he scraped up thirteen pebbles from the ground and dropped them into his pocket.

There was no way of telling whether the thirteen pebbles would do any good, but at least Kit could be sure they wouldn't do any harm. His two hits helped the Colts to a seven-to-three victory over the Bears. But it wasn't the sort of game that depended on Kit or any other single player. The Colts were clicking as a team. They were strong in every position but one. When Bill pitched, first base was again a problem.

Mr. Ginger moved Ted from second to first and put Lew on second. But Ted fell almost as far short of being a good first baseman as Ralph. This time it hadn't hurt the Colts much, but in a close contest the errors would have cost them a game.

"Great work, boys! By George, you were really

hustling today. Didn't I tell you we were going to have a winning team?" Mr. Ginger's voice was jovial and his smile was bright as he complimented his team after the game.

Kit didn't think anyone else noticed Mr. Ginger's anxious look as he glanced from player to player. Kit felt he knew what the manager was thinking. The Colts still weren't the team Mr. Ginger wanted them to be. They couldn't be without a reliable first baseman. Kit wondered which boy Mr. Ginger would try there next.

Chapter 16

Out of Action

"KIT, I'M DEPENDING on you," Mr. Ginger said.

"Oh, *no!*" Kit's wail was even more despairing than the one he had unloosed when Mr. Ginger first asked him to pitch. To play first base seemed like a big step down. On the mound the game was yours to win or lose. Behind the plate you were pretty much in charge. But at first base you didn't make anything happen. You just waited for what other people would do. Even so, it would be a tough spot. Neither Ralph nor Ted had been able to handle it, and Kit was far from sure about himself.

Glancing around, he saw that Web was busy getting Bob warmed up. "Why not Bill? He did all right at first."

"Bill and his family are out of town on a trip."

Kit groaned. "Don't blame me if I fumble everything. I never played first. I've never put on one of those silly-looking gloves."

"Then you'd better start getting used to it," Mr. Ginger said. "I know I'm asking a lot. A right-handed first baseman has to be extra fast. But you've got the speed—not only in your feet but up here." He tapped his forehead. "We have a tight defense except for that hole at first. I'm counting on you to plug it up."

Kit decided that if a first baseman was what the Colts needed most, he would try to be one. To his amazement, trying turned out to be fun. There was a freedom he hadn't had behind the plate or on the mound.

Mr. Ginger drove the ball at Kit high and low, to his left, and to his right. Kit stretched and bent and leaped and began to learn the patterns that let his feet find the bag without looking for it. As he threw to the other bases, he understood why a right-hander had to be extra fast. He needed to turn himself into position for a throw.

Kit became so absorbed in learning first base that he had no time to notice anything else. But when the Colts turned over the field to the Lions for warm-up, he saw that the bleachers were already filled with people. They were the usual crowd of parents, friends, and people from the Marley Home.

Then Kit's eyes were dazzled by something decidedly not as usual. Instead of her old black shawl, Miss Rogers was wearing a wide-brimmed hat of pale gray that was lavishly trimmed with bright purple ostrich plumes. She smiled at Kit and beckoned to him imperiously.

"Like my new hat, Christopher?" she asked.

"It's beautiful, Miss Rogers." That was an outrageous lie, but Miss Rogers looked so happy it would have been cruel to say anything else. "Did you pick our team colors on purpose?" he asked. "Or did you just happen to like that one in the shop?"

"Heavens, Christopher!" Miss Rogers laughed. "You don't think one could *buy* a hat like this! I made it."

Kit was astonished. He had never thought of anyone making a hat. "Honest?"

"Of course. You see, Mrs. Kelly decided to be a Lions' fan. Look at her!" She nodded toward a stout lady with a bow of green ribbon pinned to her dress. "So I had to think of something to show whose side I was on. But this hat's nothing, Christopher. You should see the things I used to make, like ermine cloaks for kings, armor for knights, shining robes for angels . . . "

"I'll tell the fellows you made the hat to show you're a fan of ours," Kit said hastily. "They'll appreciate it." He did, but he didn't mention the stuff she had said about making robes for kings and angels. He had heard that sometimes old people's minds got confused, and he didn't want anybody laughing at Miss Rogers.

The first three innings were a pitchers' battle. Kit felt useless as he watched Web and Bob working smoothly together. He felt just as useless at the plate, where two walks robbed him of a chance to hit. Both times he remained helplessly at first until the inning ended.

Regardless of this inactivity, Miss Rogers and a little group around her that included Mr. Benjamin and Mr. McIntyre applauded wildly each time Kit came to bat or took the field. The other Colts began to grin and make sly remarks about the Kit Dawson Fan Club.

Kit led off the fourth determined not to walk again. The pitcher was still keeping the ball away from him, but Kit lunged for an outside pitch and dropped it over the second baseman's head. The Kit Dawson Fan Club cheered, and Miss Rogers pounded the bench with her cane.

This time Kit's teammates didn't go down tamely as they had before. Ralph guarded the plate, fouled off seven pitches, and at last got a walk. Bob laid down a bunt so well that he outran the throw to first. This loaded the bases.

The Lions' pitcher began to show signs of nervousness. He glanced uneasily from base to base and ended by throwing hastily. Ted grounded the ball back toward the mound. By the time the pitcher had fielded it, Kit was sliding for the plate. The pitcher settled for getting Bob at second. Sam was put out on a grounder to first that brought Ralph in with a second run and sent Ted to third. Then a long single by Martin Woolsey drove Ted across the plate and gave the Colts a three-to-nothing lead before Bruce struck out to end the inning.

The Lions came back with two runs in the bottom of the inning, but the Colts clung to their slim lead through the fifth. In the top of the sixth Kit found himself leading off again.

This time the Lions didn't give him a chance to reach for a bad pitch. The catcher stepped aside to take four tosses. Kit watched resentfully from first while Ralph and Bob struck out. Ted popped a high fly that the right fielder took for the third out.

Kit trotted gloomily to his place off first. He wondered if anyone could be more useless than he had been in this game. Mr. Ginger had admitted that he was asking a lot of Kit by making him fill that important hole at first base. Well, here he had stood through five innings, and not a ball had touched his glove. He might as well have stayed home.

Bob struck out the first batter. Then he walked the Lions' second baseman who was so short he was hard to pitch to. Next, the shortstop grounded past third for a single. Kit began to get nervous with two on and one out.

Bob struck out the Lions' catcher and then put

the first baseman on by brushing his arm with a pitch. The bases were loaded, and Kit had had no chance to do a thing about what had happened. After this, he told himself fiercely, Mr. Ginger had better never try to talk him into playing first base again.

Next up was the Lions' left fielder, a boy known for hitting best in a tight game with runners on base. Kit groaned.

Though he had given up hope of having anything to do in the game, he glanced around and decided how he would act if he did get his hands on the ball. He stood half-crouched, alert, and loose. He was ready to move in any direction.

When the bat cracked against the ball, there was no time to think. Kit moved instinctively, sprinting back, leaping high with glove outstretched. The ball smashed into the glove with such force that for an instant it seemed impossible to hold. But Kit held it. The yell that had gone up to celebrate a hit was cut short. Then came a roar of delight at the realization that Kit's catch had ended the game.

"Boy, what a catch!"

"If I hadn't seen it, I wouldn't have believed it!"

"You saved us that time, Kit!"

The Colts pounded Kit on the back as they shouted congratulations. Kit grinned. Happiness blotted out his discouragement, and suddenly first base didn't seem like such a bad place.

Miss Rogers and the other ladies were pouring lemonade and setting out cookies. The boys talked and laughed as they helped themselves. Refreshments from the Marley Home had already become a pleasant custom.

"Didn't I say that you're the one who holds the team together?" Mr. Benjamin demanded. "Look what you did today, first time at first base."

"But there was hardly anything to do. You saw!" Kit protested.

"Sure I saw. That's the way it goes sometimes. But when something came along for you to do, you were ready and did it. That's what counts."

Again Kit felt that he didn't deserve Mr. Benjamin's praise, so he changed the subject. "Pretty nice of Miss Rogers to put our colors on her hat. She really *made* it?"

"Sure!" Mr. Benjamin said. "That's nothing for Miss Rogers. For forty years she was wardrobe mistress for the Royal Star Troupe. Grand actors, they were, who used to tour the whole country. Miss Rogers dressed everybody from Cleopatra to the Angel Gabriel."

Kit grinned sheepishly but said nothing.

At dinner Kit related with breathless excitement what Mr. Benjamin had told him about Miss Rogers. "I must have known all those people did something before they came to the Home. But I never thought about things so interesting. Just imagine, Mr. Benjamin was a real baseball player, and Miss Rogers used to make all those costumes for plays."

Kit's mother looked excited. "Oh, my! I wonder . . . No, we couldn't."

"Couldn't what?" demanded Kit's father.

"I was thinking of asking her to help with costumes for the Fourth of July pageant. Everybody's bored with those threadbare old things we've been using, but nobody in the Women's Club has any good ideas for new ones. Still, it wouldn't be right to ask Miss Rogers. At her age, she deserves to be let alone."

Mr. Dawson frowned thoughtfully. Then he said, "Why don't you ask her? She can't have lived all these years without learning how to say no."

"I will if you really think it's all right. I'll speak to her at the next game. I'll explain that she needn't do any work. All we need is someone to tell us what to do."

"You know. . . . " Kit hesitated, hoping his parents wouldn't laugh at what he was going to say next.

"What is it, dear?" His mother gave him an encouraging smile.

"I wish we could ask Great-Grandma to come and live with us. I hate to say it, but I never thought much about her before. I could never imagine anybody that old being—well, a real person like anybody else. But since I've gotten to know the

Marley Home people, I've started thinking that maybe Great-Grandma would be a good friend, too. And she might be lonesome in the city all by herself."

For a moment Kit was afraid he had said something wrong, for it seemed that his mother was going to cry. But she didn't. She said, "What a nice idea! We have asked your great-grandmother to come many times. But she always said she enjoys living as she does and being independent. But we'll pay her a visit in the fall, and we'll invite her again. Perhaps she'll change her mind. Even if she doesn't, I'm sure she'll be happy to know that you want her as much as your father and I do."

Chapter 17

A Sudden Silence

MIDWAY THROUGH the season, everyone had stopped thinking about the old field where a spreading cluster of buildings was beginning to look like a shopping center. The bleachers at the old field had been almost empty sometimes. But at the new field there was always an enthusiastic crowd.

Marley Place became so busy that it was hard to remember it as an empty and mysterious street. And all its traffic wasn't going to Little League games. Kit's mother went there to pick up Miss Rogers for meetings of the committee that was planning the Fourth of July pageant.

Mr. McIntyre, a retired minister, was driven to the church to help bring its membership records up to date and catalog its new library. He had even preached the sermon one Sunday when Mr. Adams had been called out of town. No doubt he would be asked again, since his first sermon was so well received.

Mrs. Roe, a friend of Kit's mother, discovered that Mrs. Kelly had once edited a music magazine. She persuaded Mrs. Kelly to help her with a series of children's concerts.

It was hard to believe these people had been in Millbrook all along, unnoticed by the townspeople. Now the people from the Home seemed to be everywhere, except when a game was in progress. They were always at the field during games.

Kit was grateful to all the Marley Home people for making the season possible, but especially to Miss Rogers. It was she who first spoke to him and invited him into the Marley Home. She even wore the Colts' colors on the hat she had made. Even more than Mr. Benjamin, Miss Rogers had become Kit's special friend.

The season could hardly have turned out better despite the fact that the Colts fell into a dismal slump and lost three games in a row. Kit's worry that Tom might be homesick and missing his Little League teammates had been banished when a letter finally came from the camp. Tom was having a glorious time with his new friends and was particularly elated over having just been elected captain of the camp's baseball team.

It surprised Kit to discover that winning or losing didn't make much difference in his enjoyment of a game. He felt that he was doing well playing a good first base and getting his share of hits. The slump was really nobody's fault. The Colts just weren't a very good team. Bill was a good pitcher but a poor fielder. Web was a reliable catcher but a weak hitter. Bruce was a ball hawk with a weak arm. Ted was inconsistent, Mike slow, and Ralph timid. And of late all these weaknesses had been showing up at the most damaging times.

Still, every game was a fresh chance. Mr. Ginger's bright-eyed hopefulness was undimmed by defeat. When the team gathered on a hot Saturday afternoon to play the Bears, everyone looked as cheerful as if the Colts had been leading the league.

"This is our day," Mr. Ginger announced. "I can feel it in my bones! How's the arm, Bob?"

Bob grinned. "Never better."

"Swell! You're our pitcher. Where's Sam?"

Mike, who lived next door to Sam, said, "Oh! I almost forgot. He won't be here. His mother made him go along to his aunt's wedding over in Bridgeton. She couldn't get you on the phone, so I said I'd tell you."

Mr. Ginger groaned. "And I thought my lineup was all set! Now where's our shortstop?"

The Colts stared in blank-faced silence. All season Bob and Sam had alternated at shortstop. There were no volunteers to step unprepared into that key position.

Mr. Ginger's eyes moved thoughtfully from face to face. At last he said, "Well, Kit, I guess it's up to you. Bill can play first."

This time Kit didn't bother to protest. He just grinned and said, "I'll do my best, Mr. Ginger."

The other Colts' faces brightened. "Sure! Kit can handle it," Bill said happily; and there were unanimous nods of agreement.

Shortstop was a fresh challenge. Kit found himself in the middle of everything. Fair balls could come straight at him, from left, right, or up in the air. Throws could go in any direction, and they had to be quick. There also was the matter of covering second base, so a shortstop had to be on his toes every minute. But Kit was no longer frightened by the idea of an unfamiliar position. He was proud that Mr. Ginger had chosen him and that he had the team's confidence. He threw himself wholeheartedly into learning his new job.

The game started badly when Bob hit the first batter. He gave up a walk and a hit before he settled down. The Bears had a one-run lead.

In the bottom of the first with Bob on third, Lew on first, and only one out, Kit hit a long drive. But a spectacular catch in left field made it just a long out. Bob, almost home, had to dive back to avoid being doubled off. Ralph walked to load the bases, but Bill struck out to leave the Colts still scoreless.

With two out in the second Bob grabbed for a lazy

hopper off the bat of the Bears' pitcher. It glanced off the edge of his glove and bounced toward second. Kit, sure that Bob would make the play, was badly out of position. He lunged and made a desperate grab, only to have the ball glance off *his* glove and into center field. By the time Bruce had snatched it up, the Bears' pitcher was at second.

Kit's face burned. From now on he would take absolutely nothing for granted. His carelessness had earned him an error on his very first play at short-stop, even though a final strikeout kept it from costing a run.

In the bottom of the second, Ted's strikeout was followed by singles from Web and Mike. Bob walked to load the bases, and then Bruce sent a long drive into left field. It dropped safely, and Web and Mike raced across the plate while Bob went to third. Lew laid down a perfect bunt to score Bob with a third run. Applause and cheers greeted these accomplishments.

Kit came to the plate determined to make up for his error. He waited grimly for his pitch, swung, met the ball, and ran. It was a drive much like Bruce's but even longer. Kit thought it might clear the fence. But then it started to drop, and the Bears' left fielder was in position. He pulled it in to retire the side.

Kit tried not to mind. The Colts were winning, and that was what counted. But three more scoreless innings went by with no fielding chances, and it wasn't until the fifth that he got another turn at bat. This time he dropped a looping fly just over the second baseman's head to bring in Bob. At last, things were starting to go his way!

Then came the bottom of the sixth. Bob's first pitch was slammed hard at Kit's feet, but Kit managed to grab it and throw to Bill for the out. Then the Bears' left fielder met the first pitch. He drove it just out of Kit's reach and past Bruce into the farthest corner of left field. By the time Lew had chased it down, the runner was on third. The Bears' shortstop also hit the first pitch, but he drove it straight into the air so that Web pulled it in for the second out. Bob looked ready to collapse in despair.

Time was called. Kit watched Mr. Ginger walk to the mound. Now that there was no action to distract him, Kit could feel the scorching weight of the heat. The air seemed almost too heavy to breathe.

Mr. Ginger beckoned, and Kit ran over. "Bob's worn out," Mr. Ginger said. "You'd better switch places. Just get this batter out, Kit."

"Yes, sir. I'll try."

Bob's face brightened. New energy seemed to pour into him as he handed over the ball and trotted to the shortstop's position.

Kit turned the rosin bag between his sweaty hands. A fast runner was on third. The Bears probably were remembering that they had beaten him before, so they obviously were ready to pounce. Could Mr. Ginger have forgotten his shakiness at the beginning of both his pitching starts? Didn't he realize that he was the wrong one for a spot where every pitch counted?

Kit's warm-up pitches were pretty bad. The heat and the strain of playing a new position drained his strength. But the batter was at the plate, and he had to pitch to him.

Nothing worked. Low pitches plowed up dust, and high ones soared over the batter's head. Not a pitch was even near the strike zone. The batter grinned as he strolled to first. Kit managed to get one strike on the next batter, but that was all. The bases were loaded.

The next batter was the Bears' left fielder, a good hitter who loved to hit. He would be trying for a hit, not a walk. He was death on fast balls, and Kit hadn't mastered a curve. But he had been practicing a let-up pitch. Though he had never tried one in a game, he decided to take the chance.

For the first time that day something worked the way Kit had planned. The batter swung too soon, reached under the pitch and lofted it into the air. Bob waited without moving for it to drop into his glove.

That was it! They'd won! Kit let out a shrill, exultant whoop, and then realized he had shouted into a dead silence. Where were the cheers? Didn't anybody care that the Colts had pulled out a victory when defeat seemed certain?

By the bleachers players, spectators, and officials stood crowded together with their backs to the field. There might never have been a game, for all they cared.

Scowling furiously, Kit strode toward the huddle of people. He nudged a boy in a Bears' uniform. "What's the matter with everybody?"

"She just keeled over," the boy said.

Mr. Ginger emerged from the crowd and sprinted toward the house. Kit wriggled through the mass of people and craned his neck to see. Stretched full length on the lowest tier of the bleachers was a shapeless figure.

In spite of the heat, a chill went through Kit when he recognized the shrivelled, grayish face as Miss Rogers. She lay very still. Everything about her appearance told Kit that his friend was dead.

Chapter 18

Almost a Murderer

"KIT! WHAT'S WRONG?" Mrs. Dawson's voice was anxious.

Kit didn't want her to know that he had been crying. He buried his face in the pillow and muttered, "Nothing."

Kit's mother crossed the room and sat down on the bed where he had taken refuge after running all the way home. "They took Miss Rogers to the hospital, dear," she said gently. "The ambulance Mr. Ginger called arrived quickly. She'll be all right."

Kit sat up. "Will she, really?"

"So the doctors say. She's had attacks before and has always made good recoveries. They think it was the heat that brought this on." Then Kit let his mother wipe the tears from his face.

In his heart, Kit felt sure that the heat was not to blame. Someone had told him how Miss Rogers jumped up to cheer that last out and then dropped as though she had been shot. Excitement had done it. He, Kit Dawson, had just escaped being a murderer. Miss Rogers could have died, and she still might die. Doctors don't know everything, Kit thought.

And what about the other old people? Nobody knew how many of them might have weak hearts. Mr. Benjamin or one of the others might be next. If any one of them died, it would be Kit Dawson's fault. Hadn't he been the one wanting credit for getting the Marley Home field for the Little League? What had happened today made him know that it wasn't credit he deserved, but blame.

Why, he had actually ruined the lives of those nice old people, just so that he and his friends could have fun! The Home had been their peaceful haven. Then had come the noise and commotion of Little League games at their very door. As if that weren't enough, there had come demands that they leave their retirement and go to work. Because they were too nice to refuse, they had been dragged into helping with all sorts of things.

If it hadn't been for baseball, Miss Rogers and her friends would still be enjoying their happy, healthy life. Kit felt that he would never play baseball again, not after this.

Next day, Kit wouldn't go out of the house. He felt that his guilt would show in his face.

In the morning he called the hospital and asked anxiously how Miss Rogers was. "As well as can be expected," a voice said. That could mean anything, he thought, but at least he knew that she was still alive.

Kit decided to clean up his room. That done, he started to read a dull, improving book. It would have seemed terrible to have fun while Miss Rogers was so sick.

Halfway through the dull afternoon Mrs. Dawson called, "Telephone for you, Kit."

Kit ran to answer. "This is the Community Hospital," someone said. "Miss Rogers wants to see Christopher Dawson. Can he come?"

"Right away!" Kit gasped.

Twenty minutes later, Kit stood at the door of Miss Rogers' hospital room. He would have made it in ten minutes except that his mother had made him wash, comb his hair, and change his clothes. His heart was beating so hard it seemed that everyone would hear it.

Would Miss Rogers accuse him of murdering her? No, she was too nice. Probably she was going to forgive him. If anything could make him feel worse, that would be it.

A nurse came out and said, "You may go in, Christopher."

Miss Rogers was lying propped against some pillows. Her face was very white instead of the sickly gray it had been yesterday. But she was smiling, and her eyes were bright.

"Come and sit close to me." Her weak and shaky voice was friendly. Kit perched on a chair beside the bed.

"I'm so *glad* I didn't die, Christopher," Miss Rogers said.

"So am I, Miss Rogers." Kit swallowed hard.

"I'm afraid that with that good imagination of yours you would have decided you were to blame for getting me out to something as exciting as a ball game," Miss Rogers went on. "Christopher, I'm eighty-nine years old. Any woman as old as that has already lived longer than she'd ever expected to."

"We should have let you alone," Kit choked. "All of you, I mean."

"Why, child!" Miss Rogers chuckled. "Do you have any idea how dull life was before you came along? Now don't misunderstand me. The Marley Home is a wonderful place, and everyone there is thankful to Elnathan Marley for making it possible. But you know, to be eligible to live there a person must be over seventy. And the person must be without living relatives.

"Think what that means, Christopher! None of us has a child or a grandchild or even a thirty-second cousin to write to us or come to visit. Most of our friends have already left this world. We're alone. Once we've been accepted at the Home, we're given everything we need. The money Mr. Marley left has been wisely invested, so we have no worries about food or clothing, medical bills, or anything else. We have books, television, our own chapel, and even our own little movie theater. There was no need to go out, so we never went. We might have lived on the moon for all we saw of Millbrook.

"It was terribly boring, Christopher. We took up little hobbies; but needlework, painting, and raising canaries or goldfish became dull after a while. We sat comfortably and waited to die."

"But, Miss Rogers . . ." Now everything seemed to be turned around. Kit didn't know what to think anymore.

"You rescued us, Christopher." Miss Rogers gently took Kit's hand. "You came like the Prince who rescued the Sleeping Beauty. Although none of us can claim to be beauties, I'm afraid! But when you told us the boys needed a baseball field and we realized we had idle land that was just right for one, it made us important again. We had been doing nothing but taking Elnathan Marley's gifts for so long, we were about convinced that we were of no use to anybody. Then we discovered that there was something we could give.

"We decided not to go to your games. We thought you wouldn't want a crowd of old wrecks like us looking on. But before long temptation got the better of us. And we've had such fun, cheering our favorite teams and players and talking over everything that happened.

"Then people began asking us to help with things outside the Home. Knowing we could do something useful made us feel like live people again, when we had been feeling like ghosts! This summer has been the happiest any of us has known for a long time."

By this time Kit was grinning broadly.

"If I had died yesterday," Miss Rogers said, "I wouldn't have had a chance to tell you all this. The point is, Christopher, that we've enjoyed our lives. We're still enjoying them. But we're old. We're like clocks that are running down. We all know our next tick may be our last, and we're ready for that. If one of us should die at a game, that's the way we would want it. At least we would leave life in the midst of happiness and excitement. If that should ever happen, will you try to make your friends understand the way we feel?"

"Yes, Miss Rogers," Kit whispered solemnly.

"Good!" Miss Rogers patted Kit's hand briskly. "Then I'll say goodbye for now. I think I can sleep. One more thing, they say I'll be here another week or so, but I'll surely be able to come to your last game. Try to win it for me?"

"Yes'm. I sure will!"

Chapter 19

Promises To Keep

"HERE WE GO AGAIN!" Mr. Ginger crumpled the piece of paper with the lineup written on it and started to draw up a new one. Bill had appeared with his wrist in a tight cocoon of adhesive tape. He had sprained it falling off a skateboard, he explained sheepishly.

"You can coach first base, Bill. I'd been saving you to pitch this last game. It's all right, though. I know you couldn't help it. Thank goodness it's a new week so that Bob can start.

"Kit, you've been dying to get back to catching. I'm going to give you a break. Web can take first. The rest of the lineup will be as usual."

Blissfully Kit got into the catcher's gear. It was great that Mr. Ginger had given him a chance to play where he was at his best. This was one game which the Colts absolutely had to win.

They were not contending for first or second place

as they had hoped. No matter what happened to-day, they would wind up next-to-last. They had to win because Miss Rogers was in the bleachers, just as she had promised. A look of anticipation was on her face, and Kit knew that she was remembering his promise to her.

When Miss Rogers saw that Kit was going to catch, she beamed with delight.

The Colts, home team against the Lions, started off looking great. Bob struck out the first two batters and then, after allowing a single, fielded a hard grounder and threw to Web for the final out.

But in the bottom of the first the Lions looked just as good. Bob got the only hit, and it was Kit who bounced to the mound to end it.

In the second Bob tried to shave the corners and walked the first batter. Then came a drive down the first base line that stayed barely fair for a double. Kit knew he could have caught the ball had he been playing first base.

Trying harder than ever for the strikeout, Bob gave up another walk to load the bases and then another to force in a run.

Kit called time. "Forget the fancy stuff, Bob," he urged. "Don't you know you've got eight guys on your side? Just put it over and give the rest of us a chance."

Bob shrugged, glancing doubtfully at Web on first base. "If you say so, Kit."

Kit knew that Bob had faith in his advice only because in the past it had always worked out. For a moment it seemed that it would work out again. The next batter went down swinging as Bob concentrated on getting the ball over the plate. But he had been the last in the order, the Lions' weakest hitter. The lead-off man put a drive over Web's head for another double, and two more runs were scored. Once more Kit knew that if he'd been playing first, he could have reached the ball.

Bob glared at Kit, and Kit knew that he was being blamed for bad advice. Kit wasn't convinced that his advice had been bad. He called cheerily, "Lucky hit, Bob! Keep putting them in there. We'll get those runs back—don't worry!"

Bob kept putting them in. He struck out the next batter, then fielded a low, hard drive for the third out.

Once more in the fourth, a fly ball Kit could have handled easily dropped back of Web. This time a strikeout prevented further scoring, yet Kit knew what he had to do. He had waited too long already.

"Mr. Ginger, my catching's pretty rusty. I appreciate your giving me the chance. But honestly, Web could do a better job. Do you think we could switch?" Kit asked.

"I think that's a good idea," Mr. Ginger said.

Kit wasn't too happy about moving out of his favorite position. But then with two out and runners on second and third, a drive came at him swift and straight as a bullet. He sprinted back, leaped high, juggled the ball for a moment on the tip of his glove, and held it. He knew Web wouldn't have gotten within yards of it and felt enormously happy.

In the top of the sixth came a really crushing blow to Kit's hope of keeping either his promise to Miss Rogers or the one to Bob. The Lions put together two doubles and a single to score two more runs. They now led five to nothing. Kit's happiness over his good catch had evaporated long ago. With only one more chance to make up a five-run deficit, the game was as good as lost.

As if that weren't bad enough, the day had been a personal disaster. Kit failed to get a hit while Bruce, Ted, and even little Martin had been collecting them. Three times in a row he had gone to the plate with two out and runners on base and had made the final out. The last two times had been strikeouts.

Though he tried not to think about it, he was sure that by ending the season with a game like this, he would ruin any chance he might have had to be picked for the Millbrook All-Stars. To look good on a losing team, a player had to be really outstanding. Kit had been anything but outstanding today. He couldn't even hope for another chance to improve his record, for he had been the last batter in the fifth inning.

With a feeling of gloomy resignation, Kit watched Lew guard the plate. He hit several fouls before he finally collected a walk. He hardly felt more cheerful when Ralph slammed out a double. The Lions' pitcher didn't seem to mind giving up one hit in an inning, but so far that had been his quota. When Bruce sacrificed, Kit joined in the cheers. At least the Colts wouldn't be shut out.

Then Web popped up a tricky fly that dropped between the left and center fielders and brought Ralph home with a second run. Martin drove a grounder over second, and Sam followed with one that got past the third baseman. Kit applauded, but his heart wasn't really in it. It looked as if he would be the only one on the team without a hit. And in spite of everything the Colts were still three runs behind.

But the Lions' pitcher was getting anxious. Trying to keep track of three baserunners and at the same time face Bob's eagerness to win his own game, he balked. Bob went to first and another run came in.

Suddenly Kit was jolted by the realization that he would get another chance after all. Ted was up next, and there was only one out. As he watched Ted strike out, Kit couldn't help groaning. Here it was again. For the fourth time, he was batting with two out and runners on. Three times he had let the team down. If he did it again, what a disgraceful end to his Little League career!

Kit moved slowly toward the plate. So much depended on him that he hardly felt able to move under the weight of his responsibilities. Because he dreaded looking at Miss Rogers when he had failed so miserably, he couldn't keep his eyes away from her.

To his surprise, she was smiling. When she caught his eye, she waved enthusiastically. Then Kit saw Tony grinning at him from the top row of seats. Then, from first base, Bob called, "Put one out of here, Kit. You can do it!"

Kit felt an amazing sensation of relief. It was as if an actual weight had been lifted from his shoulders. He hadn't broken any promises. He wouldn't whatever happened. He had tried, and that was all he would ever be able to do. If he failed again, that was just the way things were meant to be.

Kit grinned, feeling suddenly light and loose. He swung with carefree ease at the first pitch and drove it through the hole, not far but out of everyone's reach. Taking no chances, he stopped at first. Martin crossed the plate standing up, and Sam slid in just behind him. The score was tied. A moment later Lew hit a single that brought Bob in with the winning run. The game and the season were over.

Chapter 20

The Happiest Ending

No ONE HAD expected to have the usual family picnic at the end of the season. It wouldn't be right to ask the Marley Home people to allow it.

But there was a picnic, the best the town had ever known. The Little Leaguers and their families were guests of the Marley Home. Instead of the usual hot dogs and hamburgers, there was a dazzling variety of dishes topped off with home-made ice cream. The old ladies brought out their favorite recipes, delighted at a chance to cook again for a hungry crowd.

After everyone had helped clear the tables, trophies were presented to the winning team and the outstanding players. Kit tried not to feel disappointed at ending his Little League career without a single trophy. He didn't mind that the Colts had never been a winning team. They were great kids, and the games they lost had been hard-fought and fun. He wouldn't have traded his friends for a trophy!

But he had let himself count on collecting the hitting trophy. Until the last game, he had led the league in batting average. Then by going one-for-four while Ed Markham of the Tigers had hit four-for-four in his final game, Kit had fallen two percentage points behind. But Kit realized that that was baseball and couldn't be helped.

Most of all he had hoped to make the All-Star team. That was no empty honor, for it meant playing with the best from Millbrook against the best from other towns. It was an opportunity to help bring glory to Millbrook. But playing so badly in that last game had ruined any chance Kit might have had. He would have to settle for cheering the team that was picked and helping them in practice or any other way he could.

One after another, the names of the chosen All-Stars rang out. Markham and four others were from the league-leading Tigers. Four players were tapped from the second-place Wildcats. Three came in from the Bears. Two were taken from the Stags. That must be about all, because only fifteen All-Stars were to be picked. Kit cheered with the rest as each name was announced and each boy went forward to receive his certificate.

Then, amazingly, the voice called, "Kit Dawson, Colts!"

Kit struggled to his feet. He moved forward in a daze of blissful disbelief. But as the applause swelled and he saw the smiles on faces all around him, he knew that it was true.

Bill and Bob, Bruce and Lew, and all the other Colts swarmed around Kit. They showed no trace of envy for his good fortune, only delight.

Bill summed up the feeling. "They won't forget that the Colts are still in the league, even if they are down around the bottom of the heap. You'll show them, Kit!"

Kit grinned and blushed. "I'll sure try," he promised.

Then Mr. Benjamin called for attention. "Does everybody feel equal to walking over to the field?"

There were some good-natured groans, but nobody could refuse. Mr. Benjamin and a couple of dozen aged companions already were starting briskly off.

They hardly looked like the same people Kit had met only a few months before. It wasn't only that Miss Rogers had traded her witch-like black shawl for a purple-feathered hat and her shapeless black gown for a neat summer dress. They had all become tidy and even fashionable. But more important, they began to move in a brisk way, and their faces were lively and alert. As Miss Rogers had said, they were living instead of just waiting to die. Kit felt proud and grateful all at once.

Kit had been so busy watching his Marley Home friends that he hadn't glanced toward the field. After all, he knew what *it* was like. Then he heard cries of astonishment all around him. He looked for the reason and couldn't suppress his own yelp of delight.

In a corner of the field against the dark pines, stood a magnificent scoreboard. Across the top in big white letters was, MARLEY FIELD—HOME OF THE MILLBROOK LITTLE LEAGUE.

"A little token of friendship," Mr. Benjamin said. "You also have a standing invitation to use the field as long as you like. Of course, you might find a better place some day with more room for parking and so on. If you do, we'll pay to move the scoreboard there."

When the rush of thanks had subsided, Mr. Benjamin asked everyone to walk back to the house. So back everyone went, while the boys tried to imagine what other surprise might be in store.

Through the big gates which stood open as they nearly always did these days, came a shiny blue and white bus, the kind that carried people between Millbrook and the neighboring towns. It was empty except for the driver. Along its side was an enormous banner reading, MILLBROOK LITTLE LEAGUE OLD-TIMERS CLUB.

"You'll see that bus a lot once the tournament starts," Mr. Benjamin said, chuckling. "We've chartered it to take us wherever you go to play. It may be one game or a dozen. Whatever happens, we're one bunch of fans you can be sure of."

This was the happiest ending a perfect season could have, Kit decided. But it seemed that there was one thing more. The driver handed a package to Mr. Benjamin, who opened the box and took out a gleaming trophy. It was bigger and more beautiful than any that had been presented that day.

"We have permission from the Little League to present a special award," Mr. Benjamin announced. "An award for service and for sportsmanship. It goes to the person who introduced us to the young people of Millbrook. Before we met that person, all we knew about those young people was what we read in the papers or heard on the radio. And as you know, it's the few who misbehave who make most of the news.

"When we met one of those young people, he wasn't at all what we expected. That started us thinking that maybe the rest weren't either. We decided to help some of them by giving them a place to have fun. Then we got a real surprise. We found that we were having as much fun as the kids, and maybe more.

"Naturally, we took a special interest in the person who had started it all. As time went on, we saw him put his team's good ahead of his own. We watched him take on every tough assignment that came his way and cheerfully do his best.

"We think that is the real Little League spirit. Not only that, it's a spirit that will be valuable all through life. We want to do our bit to encourage it by awarding a trophy each year to the Little Leaguer who best demonstrates that spirit. Our best wishes to the first winner—Kit Dawson."

Mr. Benjamin put the trophy into Kit's hands. Kit knew that there were fine, impressive words of thanks that he should say, but he couldn't think of even one. Yet somehow he was sure the other Little League Old-Timers and their friends, the *real* old-timers, knew exactly how he felt.